RELENTLESS
WAKE

A JASON WAKE NOVEL: BOOK 3

MATTHEW RIEF

Cover Design by Ryan Schwarz of The Cover Designer
Line and Copy Editing by Sarah Flores of Write Down the Line, LLC
Interior Design and Typesetting by Colleen Sheehan of Ampersand
Book Interiors

ALSO BY MATTHEW RIEF

JASON WAKE NOVELS

Caribbean Wake
Surging Wake
Relentless Wake

JOIN THE ADVENTURE!

Sign up for my newsletter to receive updates on upcoming books on my website:

MATTHEWRIEF.COM

ONE

LAKE MANYARA LODGE
TANZANIA

NIKOLAI REZNIKOV SAUNTERED into the five-star
hotel's dimly lit lounge, his polished ivory cane
striking the stone floor with every step. The gray-
haired Russian wore a crisp, dark-blue suit, and
moved with the strength and arrogance of a man much
younger than his sixty years. Stopping and leaning
against the ebony bar counter, he ordered a shot of
Stoli, then let his piercing brown eyes scan the space.

Elegant African décor, with stone-embossed walls,
mahogany rafters, and ornate crystal chandeliers dec-
orated the room. Traditional artwork garnished the

scene, including a colorful, eight-foot Tingatinga painting of a herd of elephants roaming the plains.

Sweeping his eyes over the mostly empty leather chairs arranged around antique end and coffee tables, Reznikov stopped at his desired objective. Plopped down in one of the middle seats was a lanky, middle-aged man wearing a beige safari suit, and a matching pith helmet rested on the table beside him. The patron sat with his legs crossed and held a weathered first edition of Hemingway's *Green Hills of Africa* out in front of him.

Reznikov grinned, snatched the fluted shot glass from the counter, and splashed the spirit down his throat in one quick pull. Setting the glass back onto the waxed hardwood, he wiped his mustache and roamed toward the center of the room. To his right, a series of windows and glass-paned double doors provided glimpses of the veranda and a half-moon kindling the night sky. During the day, the lodge offered breathtaking views of the lake and Great Rift Valley beyond.

Reznikov stopped casually in the middle of the lounge and turned on his heels. "Julien Lestrange?" he said, feigning surprise as he pointed his cane at the seated man, who peered intelligent eyes over his book, then let out a short sigh. "Why, that is you,"

Reznikov said, chuckling as he dropped into a plush chair across from him.

Lestrange glanced back into the pages of his book. "I thought I caught a whiff of your revolting stench, Nikolai," he said in a posh French accent.

"Ah, Lestrange, still patching your fragile manhood by gunning down gazelle from afar?" Reznikov's lips formed a pretentious smile.

"Actually, it was a leopard today. What about you, Nikolai? What endangered creature have you targeted with your frail limbs and lackluster aim recently?"

Considered the crown jewel of African hunting countries, Tanzania had seen some of the most notorious hunters to ever pick up a weapon trek its plains in hopes of testing their mettle. The Russian had been hunting in Africa since he was a boy but took no offense to the jab.

"I'm surprised to see you here at all," Lestrange added. "Thought you'd be taking shelter with the other poachers in the restricted zones."

Reznikov cleared his throat. "If you must know, I've been testing myself against game that would make you cower in fear. In fact, I just returned from a four-day rhinoceros hunt in the shadow of the great Kili." He leaned back into his chair and took a gander around the room. "Thought I'd step down and mingle with the beginners for a change. Maybe teach you a thing or two. Perhaps you will join me in the big boys club one day. Provided your skills vastly improve."

"Not every man can poach an endangered species and sleep easy at night, Nikolai."

Reznikov broke into laughter, then narrowed his intense gaze. "Taking down a charging African white rhino with the snows of Kilimanjaro glistening in the sun at the beast's back is a rush that few men will ever have the guts to experience. And . . . that kind of primal standoff takes a breed of fearlessness that I wouldn't expect you to understand."

"You're a sick and twisted man." Lestrange grabbed his drink, set his book on the table, and rose. "In fact, I believe the devil himself will shudder when you join him in the lake of fire."

"He'll be lucky if I let him stay." Reznikov tapped his cane against Lestrange's knee as the man flattened his shirt. "Leaving so soon?"

"I find myself feeling suddenly nauseated," Lestrange said. "And tired."

As he strode away, Reznikov raised his voice a peg. "Have you given any more thought to my proposal?"

Lestrange stopped, snickered, and peered over his shoulder. "As I've said again and again, Nikolai, I will not part with any piece of my collection. You're wasting your time, I'm afraid."

Why

Reznikov shoved his seat back, sprang to his feet, and stomped over to the Frenchman. "It's a faded old trinket. Nearly worthless."

Lestrange smiled, then raised an eyebrow. "Not to those who know of the legend, it isn't." He held up his glass of brandy and took a slow sip, savoring the flavor as well as the anger brewing on the Russian's face. "I heard a rumor that you were getting close, Nikolai. Your obsession is finally paying off, I see. But . . . I'm afraid you will never find what you are looking for. Best to go back to scamming the masses." He patted Reznikov on the shoulder, then turned for the exit again.

His face contorted with anger, Reznikov snatched Lestrange's wrist and jerked him back. Lestrange didn't back down or skip a beat as the Russian forced him back, and he placed a hand on a holstered revolver.

The men stared intensely at each other for a moment before Lestrange said, "The only way for you to get even one piece of my collection, Nikolai, is over my dead body."

The Russian took in a slow, exaggerated breath as he shot Lestrange a scheming look and let go of the man's wrist, then wiped his own scarred chin.

As Lestrange stormed off, Reznikov set his sights toward the exit and said, "So be it."

The Russian stayed put, watching as the gentleman took two steps beyond the lounge before being grabbed by two men and dragged stealthily into the shadows. They knocked the Frenchman unconscious with a blow to his head, then each wrapped an arm under his shoulders to carry him out. Reznikov strode in front of the men as they exited the lodge via a side door, and a valet on his smoke break stared as they loaded Lestrange into the back seat of a parked Toyota Land Cruiser.

"My friends had a little too much to drink," Reznikov said to the young man, who was watching them intently, his mouth agape. After slamming the back door, Reznikov climbed into the passenger seat and shot the valet an evil side glare. "Say a word, and you're dead, boy."

The driver hit the gas, cruising them out of the lodge's parking lot. They drove deep into the rolling mountains, winding along a barely noticeable dirt road for over an hour before coming to a stop at a plateau. All around them, the tree-riddled landscape dropped off instantly to a ravine below.

The driver cut the engine and headlights, and Reznikov and his men climbed out. The night was calm and humid, the scene blanketed by a massive sea of stars set in inky blackness. The sounds of the African plains filled the air, with the roar of distant lions, arguing baboons, and scurrying critters in the surrounding brush.

The two men grabbed Lestrange and dragged him onto the grass. Reznikov splashed a bottle of ice-cold water on him, and Lestrange woke up panting as he looked around frantically.

"Where are we?" The Frenchman looked up, and his eyes adjusted until he saw Reznikov's face. "What the hell are you doing, Nikolai?"

When the Russian didn't respond, Lestrange reached for his hip.

"I'll say one thing about you," Reznikov said, inspecting Lestrange's classic Modèle revolver. "You have good taste in firearms."

Slowly, Reznikov adjusted the weapon, aiming the barrel straight at Lestrange.

"You're not gonna kill me," Lestrange spat.

One of Reznikov's men opened the back of the Land Cruiser and grabbed a slab of meat from a cooler. Lestrange watched, confused, as the guy stomped past him, stopped on the edge of the cliff, then turned back to Reznikov, who gave him a nod. Rearing the meat back, the brute hurled it over the edge, the slab striking a smooth rock face and tumbling to a stop fifty feet down.

"Why kill you . . ."—Reznikov strode slowly toward the Frenchman—" . . . when I can let Mother

Nature deal the blow." The sounds of growls and pattering paws echoed from the dark ravine, accentuating his words.

Still gripping the pistol, Reznikov grabbed Lestrange by his shirt, forced the guy to his feet, and shoved him toward the edge. "I am a reasonable man, Lestrange. I do not ask for much. I want the artifact. Give it to me, and I will take you back to the lodge, where we can drink to our agreement."

Lestrange jerked himself away. "Go to hell, Nikolai."

The Russian shook his head. "Perhaps I will meet you there."

With the pistol still aimed at the Frenchman, Reznikov planted his left leg, then struck his right heel into Lestrange's chest. The man groaned as his body flew back, the air knocked from his lungs. The blow flung him over the edge, and the experienced outdoorsman spun his body to do everything he could to stop his fall. But the rock face was too steep, and he swiftly picked up speed, smashing against jagged edges of rock before pummeling to the dirt at the bottom of the gorge. His right leg cracked from the force, and he yelled out in pain.

Fighting through the agony, the Frenchman looked up as the sound of growling carnivores filled the shadows around him. Even a starving spotted hyena would think twice before engaging a full-grown man, but in a pack, and with Lestrange injured from the fall, the hungry predators advanced.

His leg broken, Lestrange yelled as loud as he could manage and clawed desperately for nearby stones, chucking them toward the beasts. The horde of meat eaters growled back, saliva dripping from their rows of teeth as they closed in. Lestrange let out a shrill cry as a hyena lunged forward and chomped on his right calf. He managed to shake the creature off, but two more took its place, biting his shoulder and left hand. The remaining predators swarmed, gnawing at Lestrange's flesh as he howled cries that echoed for miles across the savannah.

Reznikov watched the gruesome scene unfold from his perch on the rock face above, his lips forming a crude smile.

Only now does the fool realize his folly. Only now does he understand the consequences of facing off against me.

Reznikov stood at the edge until the suffering subsided and the hyenas dragged and feasted on their portions of the kill. Turning around, he reached into his pocket, pulled out a satellite phone, and thumbed in a number. When a man answered, Reznikov said, "Sadly, Monsieur Lestrange has fallen victim to a tragic hunting accident."

"That's terrible news."

"Simply tragic," Reznikov said, peeking back down into the ravine. "And now that he is gone, I will take possession of the item I seek."

The man on the other end cleared his throat. "Per Lestrange's will, all items in his collection must be auctioned off and the funds donated to charities of his prior choosing."

Reznikov clenched his teeth. "You assured me that the artifact would be mine. You—"

"And it will. The artifact you seek is of little value. I have no doubt that you will claim it at auction with minimal effect on your pocketbook." There was a moment's pause, then the man added, "It will be yours, Nikolai. I can assure you of that."

Reznikov gripped the phone so tightly he nearly broke it. This wasn't the agreement, and he vowed to deal with this smart-mouthed lawyer in time. But first, he needed to claim the item that had been his obsession for the past twenty years.

Reznikov cleared his throat. "When and where is this auction?"

TWO

JASON WAKE DESCENDED through the crystalline Caribbean, finning along the edge of a colorful reef sprawling with marine life. Streamlining his body, he kicked smoothly and kept his eyes peeled as a school of spooked fish dispersed around him.

A glimpse at his dive computer told him he was twenty feet down. Turning his body around, he exhaled a trail of bubbles from his regulator and eyed his dive buddy, who was staring at a waterproof tablet and floating just above the sandy seafloor.

"How we looking, Finn?" Jason said through the full face mask radio.

The short Venezuelan peered up from the tablet, then pointed a finger forward. "Another hundred yards to the site."

Jason turned back forward and continued on his course. "Roger that."

Gazing at the underwater wonders around him, Jason couldn't help admiring the sheer beauty of the tropical paradise. At eighteen miles long, Horseshoe Reef is the fourth largest barrier coral reef in the world. Locals estimate that Horseshoe has claimed over three hundred vessels throughout the years, many of which were Spanish and British galleons and American privateers. The natural beauty, combined with the abundant variety of marine life and wreck sites, made the waters off Anegada one of the best places to dive on Earth.

But Jason and Finn weren't there to take in the sights.

After dealing an explosive and fatal blow to the leader of a human trafficking ring in Jamaica, Jason and the crew of the *Valiant* set their course for the northwestern fringes of the Leeward Islands to investigate reports of blast fishing. The reports clustered along Horseshoe Reef, an infamous shoal that nearly surrounds the island of Anegada. The severity of the explosions had been too great for Jason and his team of covert operatives to ignore, and they wanted to catch whoever was responsible before greater blows were dealt to the ecosystem.

Jason descended along an overhang. With little of the late afternoon sun trickling that deep, he flicked on his dive light for a better look through the deep blue. Shining the beam along the coral-coated limestone, he kicked through a narrow opening, rounded a corner, then spotted a massive crater in the rock.

His heart ticked up at the sight. An entire section of the subaquatic environment had been decimated, leaving behind a grim, barren landscape covered in sediment. Angling the beam of his dive light forward, he gasped a train of bubbles as his blue eyes focused on a row of three more craters trailing off into the distance along the reef.

"Finn, you read me?"

"Loud and clear, Jase."

Jason paused and turned away from the damage. He'd looked over the blast sites via aerial footage from their drone, but witnessing the scene firsthand hit him like a fist to the gut.

"I've reached the site."

Jason cocked his head back as Finn closed in from behind, navigating the same narrow opening.

The Venezuelan kicked until he laid eyes on the damage, then froze, clearly having a hard time believing what he was seeing. "Holy crap."

"The problem appears to be even worse than we were led to believe." Jason pointed toward the fringes of the nearest crater. "I'm gonna take a closer look." He patted his friend on the shoulder, then kicked toward the seafloor.

Jason kept his eyes peeled for any clue as to who was responsible, but his team's initial theory of local criminals with dynamite proved unrealistic. The craters were much too big for that, Jason told himself. Even from a purely logistical standpoint and throwing legality out the window, it seemed unfeasible that they'd use so many explosives. The crater easily bore ten feet into the seabed—a blast too big for simply killing fish.

Jason had read up on blast fishing while they'd motored across the Caribbean. He'd learned that the practice usually involved end-of-their-rope fishermen whose livelihoods had been decimated by commercial fisherman and needed to catch fish any way they could. While one person spotted a school of fish, the other would toss a bomb into the water, resulting in vast numbers of dead marine life.

But one look at the craters convinced him that they were witnessing the handiwork of criminals much more advanced and sinister.

After taking in the scene and snapping out of it, Finn angled his underwater camera and moved in behind Jason. "See any clues?"

"Nothing yet. . . ." They finned along the crater, then down into its center, scanning every inch of the wasteland of a crime scene. "But these guys used some heavy explosives, whoever they are."

"You could say that again. I've seen the effects of blast fishing before, but this . . . I've never seen anything like this."

They moved across the craters, filming everything and keeping their eyes peeled for clues. While examining the third and final blast site, a woman's voice came over their headsets.

"Checking in, boys," Alejandra said. "Jase, Finn, you guys still alive down there?"

"Just wrapping up the final crater," Finn replied.

"As bad as the others?"

"These are the worst yet," Jason said, "but we're coming up empty. Looks like we're gonna have to head onto the island and snoop around if we want some answers."

"Roger that. You've been down for over an hour. You both should be getting low on air."

Neither Jason nor Finn needed to glance at their pressure gauges. They were both experienced divers and checked them instinctively every couple of minutes.

"We'll surface in a minute," Jason said. "Just gotta finish searching this last site."

They skirted the perimeter, surveying and recording every detail to be reviewed after the dive. Just as Jason was about to motion toward Finn for them to surface, he spotted a shimmering object near the opening into a narrow cut in the reef, and he spun his body around smoothly and kicked. He expected it to be a shell or perhaps the sleek silvery body of a fish keeping still in the water, but as he moved closer, he realized it was a small square piece of solid metal. He dipped a hand into the sand and lifted it for closer inspection.

"You find something?" Finn said, seeing his buddy examine the object.

"A dive weight. Looks like it hasn't been here long."

"A weight? Who the hell would be diving here?"

As Finn moved closer, Jason looked up and spotted movement in what he realized was a long crevice in the rock. It was quick and far off, but Jason caught a good look and knew instantly that it was another diver.

He dropped the weight and then streamlined his body, kicking toward the crevice and weaving around thick growths of fan coral at the opening.

"What is it?" Finn said, watching Jason take off. "You see another blast site?"

Jason kept up his pace, scissoring his fins in powerful cycles. "No, but I don't think we're alone down here."

THREE

ROUNDING A SHARP corner, Jason angled his body to fit, his neoprene wetsuit scraping against the jagged rock. After squirming free into a larger space, Jason got his bearings. He was just five feet above a white seabed. Overhead, the crevice rose twenty feet before giving way to another fifteen feet of open water to the surface. In front of him, the top of the crevice closed in, enclosing the rock to form a cave.

When Finn reached him, Jason pointed toward the blackness ahead of them. "Whoever he was, he went that way."

Jason withdrew a titanium dive knife from the sheath strapped to his right calf and aimed the dive light still gripped in his left hand. Finn snatched his knife, as well, and the two moved into the cave, Jason leading the way.

"Alejandra, you there?" Jason said, keeping his gaze locked forward.

"Thought you guys were heading up," she said.

"Not yet. You see any boats nearby?"

"Horizon's mostly clear. A sailboat two miles northwest. We still got the reef to ourselves."

Not quite, Jason thought.

The cave weaved back and forth, breaking off into occasional veins too small for anything but fish to swim through. Scanning his light, Jason froze as he spotted a big set of bulging eyes staring back at him. They belonged to a goliath grouper that was larger than a refrigerator. Unfazed, the massive tawny-colored fish watched the unwanted intruders as they glided past.

"This place is like a maze," Finn said.

After a minute of weaving through the cave, Jason checked his pressure gauge. He was at three hundred psi—well beyond the recommended surface time. At his current breathing rate and depth, he had roughly five minutes before his tank would be empty.

"You sure you saw someone?" Finn asked.

"Positive."

Jason kept his knife ready and his eyes peeled, expecting, at any second, for someone to pop out from a dark crack in the rock and attack them. The cave closed in a second time, forcing them to traverse slowly and in single file. After pushing himself through, Jason saw a faint light trickling down and finned toward it. Knowing that his tank was nearing exhaustion, he rounded the corner, his mind and body on full alert.

Illuminated by beams of light from the opened-up cave, a diver came into focus. He was twenty yards off and kneeling on a seabed with his back to Jason, but the second he laid eyes on him, the diver turned around. Instead of scuba equipment, he had on a full set of black rebreather gear, which explained why they hadn't seen any of his exhalation bubbles. He was big and wore a shorty wetsuit that put his bulging muscles on display.

As the diver whirled around, Jason's attention immediately went to the dark, torpedo-shaped object clutched in the man's hands. The moment Jason's eyes rested on the torpedo, a second diver swept in from the shadows to his right. Before Jason could react, his attacker wrapped a tight arm around his throat, trying to suffocate Jason as he struggled to break free.

With just a short gasp of air in his lungs, Jason adjusted his grip on his dive knife and stabbed it into his attacker's right thigh. The man let out a cry of bubbles and loosened his grip enough for Jason to break free.

The stranger retaliated by reaching for Jason's knife through a cloud of his own blood. Just as he gripped the handle, Jason planted a foot against the rock and shoved his body toward the guy. The knife stabbed his attacker again, this time sending the blade through the guy's mask and burying it into his skull.

"Jase!" Finn yelled through the speaker.

Jason ripped his knife free, forced the man's limp body down, then turned around to engage the second diver. He saw that Finn had just reached the entrance of the cave behind him and was pointing at the diver kneeling in the sand.

Before Jason could make an attempt at taking the diver down, the stranger flicked a switch on the object, rotated his body, and shoved the torpedo through the water. A red light blinked on the object's surface as it cut through the liquid, heading straight toward Jason.

Wanting to protect his friend, and knowing that the small torpedo would enter the cave if it kept its current trajectory, Jason caught the device, spun it around, and shoved it toward the seafloor. Jason saw the diver fleeing above him, kicking with everything he had out of view over a distant wall of rock and coral. Jason bolted back into the cave, nearly colliding with Finn as they both rounded the corner.

"What the—" Finn got the words out before Jason cut him off by grabbing his BCD and twisting him around.

"Get back!" Jason yelled as they both swam like mad.

They zigged and zagged, then Jason pointed toward a cut in the rock. "Get in there, Finn!"

Small enough to fit inside, the Venezuelan squeezed into the crack, then gawked at Jason. "What about y—" Again, Finn was cut off, but this time, it was by a loud rumble that shook the underwater world around them.

Jason was only able to turn and face the direction of the noise as a surge of bubbly water raged toward him. Pounding into his body, the torrent swept Jason with it, hurling him into the chaotic vortex.

FOUR

THE SUDDEN BURST of water slammed into Jason's body, spinning him around, bashing him against rocks, and tossing him this way and that as it shot him through the cave. In the chaos of noise and bubbles and dark confusion, Jason sucked in a desperate breath from his regulator just before his BCD was ripped from his body. Rolling with a turn, he managed to slip into an adjoining cave and hold on as the powerful slug of water gushed by.

Delirious and banged up from the jostling ordeal, Jason opened his eyes, trying to take in the dark and blurry features around him. His mask and BCD were gone, and he'd lost one of his fins, but his dive light was still powered on and strapped to his wrist. Shining the beam around him, he spotted his dive gear wedged between a rock and a growth of brain coral near the mouth of the cave.

With his lungs throbbing, he swam toward his gear, ignoring the pain from the clusters of blows across his body. He reached the gear, then donned and cleared his mask before taking in a breath. The frame was cracked, allowing water to trickle in, and his tank was nearly empty. Sensing movement, he peered up into the cave just as the glow from Finn's light appeared.

"Jase!" Finn said, the damaged radio staticky as he looked over his friend. "You all right?"

"I'll let you know when I catch my breath," Jason replied, inspecting a substantial cut to his left elbow.

"Speaking of breath, we need to surface," Finn said, glancing at his pressure gauge. "Then we figure out who the hell that was back there."

Shaking the deliriousness away, Jason stared back into the dark cave through the lenses of his half-flooded mask.

Finn grabbed Jason by the arm. "Hey, you hear me? I said we need to get out of here."

"No, you need to. I'm going after that guy."

"Are you crazy? Jase, you're banged to hell, and your gear's—"

Jason didn't hear the rest of Finn's words through the static as he made up his mind, inhaled a deep breath, then clicked free his regulator and free dove back into the cave.

Jason rounded the corner and gazed upon the scene where the explosive had gone off moments earlier. A cloud of sediment settled into a crater surrounded by broken pieces of coral and rock. He saw no remnants of the torpedo or the first thug who'd tried to take him down.

Knowing that the second diver couldn't have gotten far, the former collegiate swimmer gave it everything he had, tearing through the water and closing in on his attacker. Reaching the other side of a ledge, he watched as the diver grabbed a Seascooter from the bottom and powered it on. Just before getting the propeller to spin, Jason reached the guy, grabbed him from behind, yanked his body backward, and slammed him against a rock. The man nearly matched Jason's six three, two-hundred-pound frame, and he forced Jason's arms down, throwing a fist toward his already damaged mask. The blow shattered the glass lens, and saltwater flooded the space, covering Jason's eyes.

As his assailant reared back for another blow, Jason gripped his rebreather and sliced the breathing hose. The man struggled, then kicked Jason off of him. Before Jason could make another move, the diver made a final desperate attempt to flee, grabbing the scooter and powering on the propeller. Jason tried to stop him, but the diver accelerated into the blue in a flash.

Out of air and without a mask, Jason held his hands up to protect his head and kicked for the surface. Exhaling just as he broke free, he rubbed his eyes and caught his breath while adapting to the late afternoon sunlight. The surface was calm and the water was empty around him, aside from the R/V *Valiant* anchored a quarter of a mile to the southwest.

Jason squinted toward the shore. *He must've waded in from the beach,* he thought. *Whoever this guy is, the island's his only way out of here.*

Not wanting to give his quarry any more of a head start, Jason took off, freestyling toward the shoreline. After completing just six strokes, he spotted the diver surface a hundred yards away.

Forced to come up for air since Jason severed his air hose, the fleeing aggressor looked back over his shoulder before firing up his Seascooter. He came up intermittently but rapidly reached the white sandy beach.

Jason, pushing it with every ounce of energy he had, reached the shore less than a minute after his attacker. Slogging up onto the beach, he ran past a fisherman standing in the shallows, stunned by the activity.

Jason entered a forest of palm trees and spotted movement up ahead. A motor whined, and he caught brief glimpses of an ATV through the dense growth, the diver leaning forward and cranking the vehicle inland. Scanning down the rugged footpath that ran along the coast, Jason spotted an old moped leaning against the base of a palm tree just up from the beach. With his attacker getting away, Jason took off into a sprint. As Jason had expected, the islander hadn't bothered taking the key from the ignition.

"I'll bring it back!" Jason shouted to the fisherman, who was splashing toward him while waving a fist in the air.

Jason started up the engine and hit the gas, shooting up sand as the small engine worked in overdrive. He focused his gaze forward, weaving in and out of trees before cutting through a shortcut and bouncing onto the same dirt road his attacker had used.

Following the sounds of the ATV's engine and the lingering cloud of dust, Jason gave the little vehicle everything it had, accelerating up to its max speed of sixty miles per hour. He maneuvered around potholes, bounced over roots, and ducked under overhanging palm fronds.

When he reached a straightaway, Jason spotted the ATV in the distance. With the road bending around a slight, tree-infested hill, Jason, wanting to block his enemy's escape, veered off the road and cruised right into the jungle. When the going became too thick, he drifted the moped to a stop and then darted through the forest. He broke free of the trees on the other side of the rise and saw the dirt road just below, but the ATV was nowhere in sight.

Jason listened carefully and heard the distant sound of the off-road vehicle's engine. Apparently, the driver had also turned off the road and was cruising toward the western shore of the island. Jason hustled toward the road, but by the time his feet hit the dirt, the sounds of the engine had gone silent. Following the road back, he came to a gated driveway that ran away to the northwest and was flanked by signs that read "private property" and "no trespassing."

Jason slipped past the gate and jogged down the narrow road, water still dripping from his wetsuit. He stopped to catch his breath and look around as the tropical forest opened up, revealing a short stretch of rocky beach and a private dock with a boat moored at the end. Creeping in close, Jason spotted the ATV parked in a small covered area near the base of the dock. He kept to the shadows as two men appeared from the boat and untied the mooring lines. One of them was his attacker, the muscular bald man still wearing his black shorty wetsuit.

Jason thought about sneaking aboard and dishing out his own brand of bare-knuckle justice. After the destruction he'd seen at the reef, and with the guy trying to kill him and Finn, the desire to beat his way to some answers was strong, but he wanted to know where they were motoring off to.

Taking down a few criminals is nice, he thought, watching them closely, *but I'm after the whole hive.*

As stealthily as possible, Jason moved in even closer, managing to get a good look at the white-hulled, fifty-foot Bertram convertible as it chugged away from the dock. The words "Coastal Charters" were painted in dark blue letters on the hull.

Keeping his eyes on the boat as it quickly picked up speed and motored north along the shore, Jason wiped the damp, dark hair from his forehead. With his radio long gone, he needed to send a message off to his team however he could. He trotted back to the base of the hill where he'd left his ride. Opening the plastic trunk attached to the rear of the moped, he rifled through the fisherman's stuff and found an old flip phone.

"It's good to hear your voice, kid," Scott Cooper said after answering. "You get the guy?"

"No, but I might have something even better. A white, fifty-foot fishing boat with a bridge just left a small dock on the western shore. It's hauling at over

29

forty knots, and the only way for them to go is north-west to avoid the reef."

Jason heard the tapping of computer keys on the other end, then Scott replied, "All right. We've got them. What are you thinking?"

Jason clenched his jaw as he thought over the recent series of events. "I'm thinking we track them down, give them a taste of their own medicine, and figure out what the hell they're up to."

FIVE

"**H**OW DO YOU feel?" Alejandra asked as Jason leaned the moped against the palm tree where he'd found it.

He rotated his sore shoulder, feeling the aches and pains up and down his body. "Like that slab of beef Rocky Balboa used as a punching bag."

The tall, athletic Latina in tight black pants, boots, and a tank top hopped out of a black rigid hull inflatable boat Finn had piloted onto the beach. Her Walther 9mm handgun was holstered to her right hip.

"Yeah, that guy looked tough," Finn said, jumping ashore.

Jason examined his torn-up wetsuit and bruised body. "It was more the raging slug of water from the explosion that did it. Now I know what it's like to be flushed down a toilet."

"Scottie said he got away as we were deploying the RHIB," Finn said, scanning over the island.

"Not for long," Jason said. "And when we figure out where he's running off to, we're gonna pay him and his friends a visit."

"Speaking of friends . . ." Alejandra said. She motioned up the beach toward the fisherman stomping across the sand toward the group.

The local looked to be in his fifties and had a lean, wiry build, but that didn't stop him from calling Jason every name in the book.

Jason broke off from the others, holding his hands out and apologizing as he strode toward the angry islander. He'd planned on paying the guy for his little joyride on the moped, but as he made his way across the beach, he noticed his attacker's red Seascooter resting in the sand.

Jason snatched the expensive gadget from the beach and held it out as a peace offering to the local.

"You're lucky you drove off so fast. I nearly put one between your shoulder blades," the man said after Jason gave a brief explanation. He lifted his shirt, revealing a Colt 1911 handgun. "Two things I never go anywhere without: my pole and my piece."

"Seems like an odd place to be armed," Jason said, scanning the empty beach.

"Yes, but there are odd people, and odd things happen—like strangers chasing each other up the beach. Better to be ready."

Jason shot him a friendly smile. "No arguments here. You seen or heard of any other odd activity around here lately?"

"I fish here every day. I never miss. Even on Christmas, I fish, and it's usually quiet here. I've heard about explosions in the water, but the reports were all at night before. This is the first time I've seen anything like that in the day."

Jason listened to the man carefully as he stared beyond him toward the other side of the island. "I'm planning to explore the island today. Any recommendations?"

The local's expression brightened. "I recommend *everywhere* on my island, but meet me at Potter's by the Sea in Setting Point later on, my friend. I'll call Henrietta and let her know. She's running the place while Liston's away. Very nice lady. And her cook is one of the best on the island. We can talk more. I'm Sherwin, by the way. Sherwin Lettsome. My family's lived here three generations."

Jason shook his hand and gave his name. "I'll see you at Potter's."

The man tipped his cap, then Jason turned and strode back toward Finn and Alejandra, who were still standing beside the RHIB.

"What the hell did you say to him?" Finn said, shocked by the fisherman's 180-degree mood shift.

Jason helped them shove the RHIB back into the water, then they climbed aboard.

"I just gave him a fancy, brand-new Seascooter," Jason said with a grin. "Seems fitting after what its former owner did to us."

Finn started up the engine and motored them away from the island, bouncing softly over the calm water. He piloted them toward the *Valiant*, a two-hundred-foot research vessel with a dark blue hull and a towering white superstructure. By all appearances, it was an ordinary research vessel with stern and side A-frames and winches and a five-ton deck crane aft of the bridge.

Finn piloted the small craft toward the *Valiant*'s stern, easing back on the throttle as a large door hinged open. He cut the engine as the rigid hull made contact with a rubber conveyer belt that gripped the boat and pulled them into the ship. The three climbed out as the door eased shut behind them.

The RHIB deployment room was wedged between the engine room below and the main deck overhead. Though ordinary on the outside, a peek beneath the exterior would reveal that the *Valiant* was one of the most unique and sophisticated vessels to ever make waves. Inheriting a fortune from his corrupt father, Jason had spared no expense on the ship's construction, giving his newly formed covert team an advanced base of operations for their unique missions.

After securing the RHIB, the three headed forward through a watertight door, then down a stairway that led into the central deployment room—or rec room, as the crew usually called it. The largest room on the ship contained an eighteen-by-twelve-foot moon pool in its center and had every piece of dive equipment imaginable. A state-of-the-art minisub rested on the port side, and a custom, amphibious aircraft with its wings folded up sat on the starboard side, rapidly deployable via a custom side door.

Jason patted down his hair with a towel and unzipped the back of his wetsuit. Peeling off the tight neoprene revealed two significant cuts—one to his side and the other to his left elbow.

Their resident dive technician inspected what remained of Jason's ravaged scuba equipment. "At least you made off better than your gear."

Jason patted the specialist on the back. "Good thing we buy in bulk." He slipped off the rest of his wetsuit as the forward door opened.

Scott Cooper, a tanned, athletic man in his early forties, strode in wearing a button-up shirt and slacks. Having served as a senator representing the state of Florida for the past six years, and having been a Naval Special Forces commander, Scott possessed a brand of confident leadership ability that few men ever reach. "Good to see you both in one piece," he said, looking Finn and Jason up and down.

"All thanks to Jase's deflection skills," Finn said. "We'd have been blown sky-high had that little torpedo from hell hit its mark."

"Not quite the welcome to the Virgin Islands I was expecting," Jason said. "But at least we know we're in the right place."

"And that we're already pissing off the right people," Alejandra added.

Scott motioned toward the door he'd entered from. "We're tracking the boat, and it's currently heading southeast. Come on up to the command room. We have a lot to discuss." He examined Jason's injuries. "Head to the medical bay first. Get all of that looked at."

Twenty minutes later, when Jason entered the command room just aft of the bridge, he saw Finn,

Alejandra, and Scott huddled over a table. At their back, a wall of monitors displayed various charts of the area and information regarding their current endeavor. On the biggest monitor, Jason saw a bird's-eye image of the fifty-foot Bertram convertible he'd asked Scott to track, its white hull cutting across the open blue in real time.

"We've got the drone locked onto it," Scott said, seeing where Jason was looking.

Jason's unique financial situation and Scott's connections allowed them to get their hands on the most advanced gadgets in the world. Their high-tech surveillance drone had electric turbine engines that could propel it up to three hundred miles per hour, and thanks to brand-new innovative batteries and solar panel wings, it could fly at cruising speed for two days without needing to recharge. It had a design similar to the General Atomics drones used by the Air Force, but it was much smaller and lacked the explosive payloads.

Jason strode over to the table and surveyed a series of images on a tablet. "That explosive device that sent me on the water park ride from hell was high-end," he said. "And the well-trained diver I chased down also had impressive gear. He clearly knew we were coming and didn't want us to investigate the blast sites."

Finn nodded. "I've encountered blast fishing poachers off Venezuela. They use whatever they can find to blow the reef and collect their fish. It would be a waste for them to use expensive, high-tech explosives."

"So, safe to say, these aren't ordinary poachers," Alejandra said.

"I don't think they're poachers at all," Scott said.

Alejandra shook her head. "But why else would they blow up the reef?"

Jason rubbed his chin. "Good question. But Scott's right. These aren't local criminals just trying to make quick illegal bucks. These guys are well organized and sophisticated."

"And, as you mentioned, well trained," Scott said. "Not many men could face off against Jase here and walk away. Or, in this case, run away."

Jason nodded in agreement. "He was fast and strong and very comfortable in the water."

Using a tablet and the touchscreen table in front of them, they reviewed satellite images of the reef surrounding Anegada, marking off locations of the twenty blast sites from the past month. There were enough to do serious damage to a fragile and pristine ecosystem.

"I'll keep going through our intel, and I'll keep an eye on these guys," Scott said, motioning toward the middle monitor. "Wherever they're running off to, it should provide us with more clues as to what they're doing here."

"In the meantime, I'll head back down to the blast sites," Finn said. "See if I can find any remnants of that torpedo or of the guy who was blown up. You up for another dive, Jase? I think there's a BCD in the rec room that you haven't destroyed yet."

"The thanks I get for saving your skin." Jason chuckled. "I'll pass. I think it's time to head ashore and see what we can learn from the locals. Besides, the island seafood's calling my name. Care to join me, Al?"

"You really think that's the best move?" she said. "That boat could hit land any minute."

Jason shrugged. "Scott will notify us when it does. And you remember Brac?" he added, referring to their romp on the Cayman Island. "Sometimes the best way to find answers is by asking around."

"I guess it couldn't hurt," Alejandra said. "At least there are no cliffs on Anegada for you to drive over."

As they left the room, Jason patted Finn on the back. "Stay vigilant. I don't think those guys are gonna return anytime soon after what happened, but you never know."

SIX

AFTER A QUICK shower and change, Jason and Alejandra motored the RHIB northwest to the other side of the island. During their voyage to the Virgin Islands, Jason and his team had researched everything they could find about Anegada. At fifteen square miles, it's the second largest island in the BVI, but one of the most sparsely populated. The tropical paradise is also the only non-volcanic island in the chain, composed instead of coral and limestone and topping out at just twenty-eight-feet in elevation.

They'd read that the island was a haven for tourists looking for quiet, secluded beaches, and that the unique destination had been growing in popularity over the years. They'd been expecting to find visitors kiteboarding and snorkeling along the perfect beaches, but the place looked deserted.

Alejandra scratched at her forehead. "I know Anegada's known for being off the beaten path, but it looks like a ghost town."

They motored up to Setting Point, tying off to a public dock beside where the walk-on ferry runs from nearby Tortola. Both of their stomachs growling from the day's activity, they headed straight for Potter's by the Sea, a colorful restaurant with seating right over the water.

Various nation and state flags hung from the ceiling, and stickers covered many of the structure's support beams. It was the kind of place Jason liked to frequent—relaxed beach restaurants where you could be sitting across from a movie star or a homeless person and no one would care less either way. It's almost like neutral territory, or a sovereign state, where you can act however you want to act so long as you're respectful.

Fortunately, the Caribbean—their home base of operations for the past six months—was full of places like that: havens for sailors and beach bums and people from all walks of life. He'd found that each populated island had its own unique version that was both familiar and distinguished by its own brand of idiosyncrasies.

A middle-aged woman with a ready smile escorted the pair to a lime green table over the water. As she straightened her waist apron over her pink T-shirt bearing the restaurant's name, she introduced herself as Henrietta. When Jason mentioned his name, it was as if a light bulb went off in her head.

"Sherwin called me and said you'd be stopping by," Henrietta said, dropping two menus down in front of them. "Said you were out diving the reef."

Jason picked up a menu. "It's one of the liveliest and colorful that I've seen."

"I just hope it'll stay that way," Henrietta said, gazing out over the blue. "If you're thirsty, I make a mean Painkiller . . . or just about anything else you'd like."

"That sounds appropriate," Alejandra said, eyeing the bruises and cuts to Jason's arms. "I'll have a Cooper Island Turtle."

Henrietta nodded, then looked over the scrapes. "Did our coral do that?"

"It tag-teamed with your limestone."

"Gotta be careful. The currents are strong around here."

Jason nodded. "You have no idea."

She laughed and patted him on the back. "One beer and a Painkiller. Extra strength." She winked at him, then strode off to the bar.

Jason and Alejandra took in the view, peering out over the bay dotted with a handful of sailboats. To their right was a long arcing stretch of beach with a spaced-out strand of docks.

Henrietta returned with their drinks, and Jason savored the blend of rum, pineapple juice, orange juice, and coconut. "Perfect," he said.

"Mm-hmm. It was invented over at the Soggy Dollar Bar on Jost Van Dyke."

As Jason sipped the drink and relished the warm effect on his battered body, he rotated his shoulder, then examined the stitches on his left arm. Jason pushed himself hard, and he often leapt without looking. At times, he even appeared to be a man who wished for death to come knocking on his door.

Seeing the worried expression on Alejandra's face, he could tell she wanted him to dial it down a peg— that for their operation to succeed, they needed him. But she didn't say anything.

Everyone has their ways of coping, and Jason had a lot to cope with. It had been less than eighteen months since his fiancée had been murdered by terrorists— since he'd only been able to watch as she died in a fiery explosion in Paris. To deal with the pain, Jason, then a former college athlete and recent graduate from Columbia, dedicated his life to exacting revenge on those responsible. For a year, the former collegiate swimmer trained at one of the most secretive and effective covert training facilities on Earth—a place simply known as Tenth Circle, as in Dante's Tenth Circle of Hell.

When Henrietta returned to take their food orders, Alejandra inquired as to the freshness of their lobster.

"As fresh as it gets," proclaimed a voice from the kitchen. A young man flip-flopped into view, his arms bulging from his cutoff shirt and his bright orange shorts covered in food stains.

The chef, who they learned was named Elvis, wasn't kidding. After Jason and Alejandra both ordered the tasty crustacean, he skipped down to the beach and called for their attention before grabbing a nylon rope and tugging a lobster trap to shore. The metal cage was packed full of the tasty bugs, and Elvis pulled two out before putting the trap back into the water.

"The two biggest of the bunch!" he said as he carried the two monster spiny-tailed lobsters onto the porch.

Elvis fired up the grill and had the two tails plated alongside red potatoes and split limes. He left them containers of melted butter, but the meat was so juicy and sweet and tender that they ate most of it by itself.

"You know . . ." Alejandra said as she washed down her bite with water. "Just once, I'd like for us to chase down bad guys someplace nice."

Jason nearly coughed mango juice out his nose. "I'll keep that in mind next time we're picking a project."

As they finished up, a moped cruised up to the front of the restaurant, and Sherwin hopped off. Striding up the wooden steps, he threw a wave to Jason and Alejandra and beamed when he saw them.

After greeting the two employees, he sauntered over to their table. "What did I tell you?" the local said, peering at their empty plates. "Amazing, huh?"

"Best lobster I've ever had," Alejandra said.

Jason pushed back one of the chairs, and Sherwin happily plopped down beside them. "In all the Caribbean, nobody grills up a bug like Elvis. The man's a wizard with those red coals and tongs." Sherwin leaned in closer and lowered his voice. "Just don't ask him to sing for you," he said, slapping his knee. "That always gets Henrietta riled up."

"Why's that?" Alejandra asked.

"Because it makes this place clear out faster than a lobster spooked from its hole." Sherwin burst into a fit of laughter.

"You keep joking like that, and I'll convince the lady of the house to tally up your tab," Elvis said from across the room. "You've been eating here almost every day for what, fifty years now?"

"I pay my way in fresh catch," Sherwin said, waving his friend off. "And you have to admit, you can't hold a tune to save your life."

"I'll have you know, I'm very good after dark"—he grinned and winked at the group—"once everyone's had enough to drink." Elvis held out his hands. "And where's this fresh catch you speak of?"

Sherwin brushed off the comment. "No catch today." He eyed the two island visitors, then lowered his voice again. "A powerful shake and a blasting spout of water scared all the fish away."

"Any idea who they are?" Jason asked, getting right to the guts of it. "The poachers?"

Sherwin shook his head, then rubbed his beard. "We've had problems here in the past, but this is different. Far worse. Far more frequent. And whoever they are, they're hurting us bad."

"The loss of fish?" Alejandra said.

"That's part of it. But few tourists will visit with the threat of danger. Not that we ever got many anyway compared to the other islands, but we rely heavily on the few we do get. Two of the island's restaurants have already closed. And the ferry from Tortola has only been running once or twice a week, while it used to run twice daily. And we've lost a lot of the sailing crowd." He pointed out over the bay, which had half a dozen sailboats anchored. "That bay's usually a sailor's commune. Boat's packed in. Foreigners coming and going, buying supplies and food from the island. With no work, and with the fishing and lobster industry affected by the blasts, locals will eventually have no choice but to leave Anegada."

"Who's investigating the blasts?" Jason said.

The man's body shook. "We've been told that agents from the Royal Police Force are investigating the issue. They motored out here a couple of times, asked questions, looked around. Then they left." He hunched over and planted his elbows on the table. "If you ask me, I'd say they were just *acting* like they were trying to help. I think there's something really shady going on. Big money. Under the table. Real shady stuff."

"You spreading your propaganda again, Sherwin?" Henrietta said, listening in as she strode across the dining area.

The local threw up his hands. "Well, somebody's gotta speak the truth around here. I'm not saying the agents and officers are bad. Hell, they're mostly fellow islanders. But the higher ups . . ." He shook his head again. "I just think something fishy is going on. And I'm not saying this as fact, but we all know the suits want us out of here and that they're willing to pay big-time money for it."

"The suits?" Alejandra said.

"Businessmen who want to buy up most of the island," Henrietta said. "They come here now and then and survey the area. Even done a few presentations for locals to attend."

"What kind of presentations?" Jason asked.

Henrietta rolled her eyes. "How our lives will be *so* much better if we sell."

"How our lives will be so much better when they turn this place into a big shiny circus!" Sherwin exclaimed. "They wanna turn it into the run-of-the-mill port town for cruise ships. Margaritaville . . . Hard Rock Café . . . the works. Anegada's perfect because it's authentic. They wanna take that away and make it a big outdoor mall."

"Any idea who these suits are?" Alejandra asked, raising her eyebrows.

Sherwin shrugged. "They all look alike. Business types that talk fast and know about a hundred words combined."

"But they've been trying to buy up our land for a while now, and they can't have it unless we agree on it," Henrietta said. "But that's never gonna happen. There's no amount of money that could make us leave, and there's nowhere else we'd rather live."

Jason thought over her words, then admired the pristine beach and aqua blue surf. "Can't say I blame you. Why leave when you've found perfection?"

The woman grinned. "I like this man. He knows a good thing when he sees it."

SEVEN

"**Y**OU TWO STAYING for dessert?" Henrietta said, shifting away from the touchy subject. "I make a mean Bushwacker."

Jason smiled. "We'd love to, but we'd like to see the island while it's still light out. You know where we can rent a car?"

"No need," Sherwin said, waving a hand. "You two can ride with me. Besides, I need to give you the royal tour, remember?"

Alejandra chuckled. "I'm not sure we can all fit on your scooter."

Sherwin pushed back his chair. "Believe it or not, I've got an old Moke. Two hundred thousand miles, and most of them right here on the island."

Jason and Alejandra paid, thanked Henrietta and Elvis, and strode out alongside Sherwin. They followed the local down the street, then climbed into his yellow Mini Moke convertible. The bubbly Anegadean drove the small vehicle onto the island's only road. Cutting around the eastern tip of the island, he motored parallel to the beach, telling them all about his island paradise while pointing out packs of flamingos wading in the island's many ponds. He showed them all the popular spots on the small island, from local hangouts to the renowned Anegada Beach Club.

"Anegada is known as the 'Sunken Island,'" Sherwin explained. "Low elevation gave it that moniker. Because it's vertically challenged and nearly enclosed by Horseshoe Reef, it's racked up quite the sunken ship count over the years."

"I'd heard over three hundred," Jason said from the back seat.

"A low estimate. Probably much more."

Sherwin drove right onto the beach near a restaurant called Flash of Beauty located on a picturesque point nestled between a calm bay on one side and waves crashing against a reef on the other. It was one of the most beautiful places Jason had seen in all of the Caribbean.

Putting the vehicle in park, Sherwin stepped out, closed his eyes, and took a deep breath of the fresh ocean air. "You two feel it yet?" he said, keeping his eyes shut as Jason and Alejandra climbed out.

"Feel what?" Alejandra said.

"The island. Its heartbeat. This place is magical. It's more than just an island, it's . . . vibrations. The kind of place that touches your soul." He took another deep, appreciative breath. "Not a lot of places like this left, and we need to protect it at all costs." They watched as the philosophic local scanned along the northern coast, then pointed out toward the reef. "They sure are beautiful, but like I was saying in the car, hundreds of ships, some of them loaded down with all sorts of treasures, crashed into those beautiful reefs."

"Ever find any of it?" Alejandra asked.

The islander grinned. "If I had, I wouldn't tell you. Beautiful as you are, miss."

Alejandra chuckled.

Sherwin picked up plastic bags of meals in Styrofoam containers from a waitress at Flash of Beauty and carried them back to the car.

"Not sure I can eat any more," Jason said, rubbing his belly.

"They're for friends of mine," the man said, loading the bags into the back of the Moke.

They hopped back into the car, and Sherwin continued driving them along the coast. He cut south, entering the island's only town, The Settlement, where most of the island's three hundred residents lived. Little more than a small grocery store and scattered simple wooden houses, the beachfront community was surprisingly active.

While driving through, Sherwin pulled into the Claudia Creque Education Centre, the only school on the island. The local grabbed the bags of food he'd brought from Flash of Beauty and strode toward the structure. A group of kids ran out, each of them excited to see the local as he divvied out the food. A woman kissed Sherwin on the cheek, then he climbed back into the driver's seat.

"That's nice of you," Jason said.

"Least I can do. Times are tough for many right now. Besides, those who can help have the responsibility to help."

Sherwin wrapped up the tour with a drive to the southeast point, turning around near the beach where Jason had taken his moped just hours earlier.

Winding along one of the island's only hills, Jason pointed out the private driveway with the closed gate flanked by no trespassing signs. "Who lives there?"

"No one, anymore," Sherwin said. "Used to be a house there years ago, but it was destroyed in a 'cane. The owner sold the place a few months ago, and the new owner's rarely there. Some kind of charter, I hear."

Sherwin fell silent a moment, then cleared his throat. "You two wanna tell me who you really are?" he said, catching them both off guard. "Remember, I watched everything. The explosion, and after that, your boat getting sucked into that research vessel. Then I asked around. It's a small island, and word travels fast. I found out you were part of the Ocean Revival team." He regarded Jason through the rear-view mirror. "But you two don't seem like environmentalists, especially when I first saw you, man. Running out of the water and chasing down a poacher with reckless abandon." He chuckled. "No, you're not like any scientist type I've ever met before."

"Jason's very passionate about protecting marine life," Alejandra said.

"I'll say." The man laughed even harder and swerved a bit, nearly taking them off the narrow road. "Passionate—that's one word for it. *Crazy* was the word that popped into my mind when I saw it. Not that there's anything wrong with a little crazy now and then. The world needs it."

"Happy to provide it," Jason said, patting the islander on the shoulder.

The Ocean Revival Project was a cover Jason and Alejandra's team used when operating around the

Caribbean. It allowed them to help the marine environment, aid locals in need, and it provided a good alibi while they tracked down criminals.

"We really appreciate the donation," Sherwin continued, referring to the funds the team had sent to aid local environmental relief efforts.

Jason raised his eyebrows, sensing that the man wanted to say more. "But?"

He sighed. "But it only does so much good. What we need are people to come in and put an end to these poachers." Sherwin slowed into a turn, then accelerated and peered out over the landscape. "Which is what I think you two are really here for."

Jason and Alejandra fell silent, thinking over the local's words. He was smart, and Jason knew there was no sense trying to deny any of it.

"Maybe you could do us a favor and keep that conclusion to yourself," Jason said. "As you said, it's a small island. We operate better when we're under the radar."

Sherwin smiled. "Your secret is safe with me."

On the drive back to Setting Point, Jason received a text message from Scott.

Boat reached its destination. Need you both back *ASAP*.

When they passed through The Settlement, Jason had Sherwin pull over at the island's only grocery store, a simple establishment with just four rows of food.

"Is the owner an honorable person?" Jason said, motioning toward the store.

Sherwin looked confused but nodded. "Yes. Very much. He's doing what he can, too, but times are tough for everyone. It's not a food bank."

The group headed into the store and met with the owner. Casually, Jason offered to buy all of the items currently in stock, as well as the next two shipments of food.

"Will that give all the people enough food for a few weeks?" Jason said.

The store owner was brought to tears. "More than enough," he said, wrapping his arms around Jason.

Back in the car, Sherwin paused a moment before putting the vehicle in gear. "I'm not sure what good graces or heavenly tides brought you to this island, but thank you."

"Like you said, those who can help have a responsibility to."

Sherwin drove them back to Potter's, where Henrietta had a stack of meals for them to bring back to the crew of the *Valiant*. Their research vessel had a nice galley and a chef they'd met in Trinidad who cooked some of the best food around, but they couldn't be the only ones to dine on fresh lobster that day.

"I appreciate all that you've done," Sherwin said. "And it is more than you had to, of course. But this problem will not be solved by money alone."

Jason untied the RHIB's stern line. "I know." He shook Sherwin's hand and thanked him for the hospitality.

"Where are you going?" Sherwin asked.

Jason fired up the outboard. "To get to the bottom of this mess."

EIGHT

BACK ON THE *Valiant*, Jason and Alejandra dished out the food, then headed straight for the command room. As they entered, they saw Scott and Finn staring intently at the main monitor.

After they shut the door and settled in, Scott pointed at the screen. "The criminals tied off here at the base of this cliffside house. We were able to zoom in with the drone and watch as two guys trudged up the steps and entered." He touched the controls on the table in front of him, playing the feed of the two men as they walked up the steep stairway and disappeared into the house. "Hasn't been any activity since."

"Which island is that?" Alejandra asked.

"Saba."

"The famous 'Unspoiled Queen,'" Finn added. "The volcanic island that boasts the highest elevation in the Netherlands."

"Can you figure out anything else about that house from online records?" Jason said.

Scott shook his head. "Not yet. There's no record of it that we could find, but we've got Murph working on it."

Elliot Murphy was a brilliant hacker and inventor friend whose skills they'd utilized time and time again. Clever as he was mysterious, the computer whiz had played pivotal roles in their taking down terrorists in the Caribbean, months earlier, as well as their tracking down illegal mining operations after that. Scott had been working with the notoriously discreet hacker for years.

"That's not all," Scott said, giving Finn the floor.

Jason leaned against the side of the table and folded his arms. "I'm guessing the second dive of the day was a little less life-threatening?"

"Yeah, but far more informative."

"What'd you find?"

Finn grabbed a plastic tub from the counter at his back and set it on the table. It contained various pieces of charred metal, along with remnants of the dead guy's dive gear. "We were right about this torpedo being advanced. We've identified this as part of the device's outer shell, and it's composed of a variety of steel alloys. This thing wasn't cheap, and certainly not an explosive worth ruining just to net some fish."

"And then there's the footage." Scott tapped a remote button that caused the center screen to transition to a paused video feed.

Jason raised his eyebrows. "Footage?"

"From my camera," Finn explained. "It was left on the whole time, and turns out, it caught a good look at the first guy who attacked you."

Scott played the feed, displaying jerky images of Jason's fight with the diver who'd pounced on him from behind. He paused the video just after Jason stabbed the guy's thigh and pushed him off, giving a side view of the criminal.

Using the remote, Scott zoomed in on the diver's exposed forearm, then focused the blurry image. A black tattoo covered part of his pale skin. Moving closer to the screen, Jason realized that it was an image of the Grim Reaper, and under the image was a line of text.

Jason tilted his head. "Looks Russian."

Scott nodded. "And it is. It's Russian for 'Death is Always Near.'"

"More than a little ironic," Finn said.

"We were able to discover the significance of this through some easy research," Scott said. "Apparently, the Grim Reaper is a popular tattoo among the Russian criminal underworld. In fact, inmates supposedly use tattoos like this to signify their status within their organization."

Alejandra rubbed her chin. "So, why are Russian criminals blowing up a reef in the Virgin Islands?"

"And trying to kill us?" Finn added.

Jason's eyes narrowed, and his brow creased as he thought over everything they'd seen and everyone they'd met that day.

"Something on your mind, kid?" Scott said.

Jason pinched his bottom lip. "I was just thinking about our conversation with Sherwin," he said, glancing at Alejandra.

"Sherwin?" Scott said.

"A local we met," Jason explained. "He's the one who let me borrow his moped earlier," he added with a smile. "He met with us for lunch, then gave us a tour of the island. He said a group of rich businessmen have been trying to buy up the island and that the recent blast-fishing incidents have affected local fishing and turned off tourists from visiting to such an extent that some locals are faced with difficult choices. It could be just a coincidence, but it sure seems like they could also be linked, especially given the sophistication of that explosive."

Finn wiped the hair from his brow and leaned back against the wall. "You really think a bunch of rich guys would go through the trouble of setting off explosions all over the reef just to get the islanders to leave?"

"And wouldn't that be more than a little counterproductive in the long run?" Scott said. "That is, if these businessmen were interested in turning Anegada into a prime tourist spot with a major cruise ship port, foreign restaurant chains, and sprawling resorts." He shook his head. "Blowing away the island's main attraction seems like a terrible business move to me."

Jason shrugged. "Depends how bad they want it. The locals I met said these rich people have been at it for a while now."

"Growing desperate," Alejandra said, nodding as she climbed aboard Jason's train of thought.

The group fell silent as they each wrapped their heads around the situation.

Finn broke the quiet after a minute by unscrewing a bottled water and taking a long pull. "Rich guys trying to buy up an unspoiled island, spikes in underwater explosions, and Russian killers," he said. "I feel like we're finding nothing but more questions as this day goes on."

Jason leaned forward, resting his hands on the table. He looked up at one of the side monitors that still displayed the drone's footage of Saba and the dock where the boat was tied off. "There's one place where we can find some answers. And something tells me we'd better move fast or this window's gonna close on us."

NINE

IF THE ISLAND of Anegada had a polar opposite, it would be Saba. Situated roughly a hundred miles southeast of Anegada, the Dutch volcanic island sprouts nearly three-thousand-feet above the dark blue surrounding it. No reefs fortify its perimeter, and the steep landscape cuts straight into the water, which sinks to over six-hundred-feet deep—just a stone's throw offshore.

But Jason spent only a moment taking in the beautiful, moonlit scenery as he hung over the edge of a cliff two hundred feet above the ocean. A warm breeze whipped against him as he adjusted his harness then contorted his body for a good look at the cliffside house below. He grabbed a pair of night vision binoculars and zoomed in on the white two-story residence that overlooked Ladder Bay on the island's western shore.

The simple concrete structure was nearly covered by trees and shrubs, making it blend into its surroundings. He traced the sets of stairs to the dock, where the fifty-foot boat was still tied off, its fiberglass hull rubbing against the fenders with each passing roller.

Adjusting his view, he gazed up along the private driveway with a gated dirt road that cut along the edge of Great Hill. From his angle, Jason could only see one other house, and it was far off to the northeast, making the cliffside structure one of the most secluded residences on the island.

"No visible activity," Jason said into his radio.

"Did a flyover with the drone and didn't see anything, either," Scott replied through the speaker. "Guess these guys aren't too worried about visitors."

Jason adjusted his grip on the taut nylon rope that extended overhead, the other end of it secured via a grappling hook to the base of a lone guava tree just out of view.

"Al, you in position?"

"Planting the package now," she replied. "Just give the word."

"Roger that. Finn?"

"Ready. Could be at the dock in under a minute."

"Copy." Jason tilted his body around and gripped the rope with gloved hands. "Moving in."

Holding on tight, Jason pushed his boots against the rock face, suspending his body off the mountainside, then he loosened and zipped down and pressed his feet into the rock again as gravity swung him back. Stopping twice on the way, Jason rappelled down the rock face, entering the shadowy, tree-covered canopy and planting his boots into the grass near the base of the house.

After looking around and not seeing any movement, Jason gripped a remote in his pocket and looked up. He'd been using a self-releasing grappling hook, which had a mechanical release that allowed the hook to be retrieved from afar. When he pressed the button, the hook collapsed into itself, and he caught the lightweight device as it fell toward him. It was just one of many innovative designs created by their team and Murph.

After coiling up the rope, Jason strapped it and the hook to the side of his backpack, then moved around to the side of the house for a better look. He stuck to the shadows as he observed the exterior of the structure, keeping his eyes peeled for any sign of movement. By all appearances, the place looked deserted—no sounds or signs of life. If it weren't for the clear sky and the silver moon glowing overhead, he'd barely be able to see that there even was a house without use of his night vision. But Jason knew that looks can be deceiving, and that at any moment, someone could pop out and attack his blind side, just like the diver had done earlier that day on the reef. Whoever they were tracking, it was clear they weren't to be underestimated.

After sneaking around the house and examining it from every angle, Jason climbed back, then shuffled around a row of bushes. With just a patch of grass between him and the house, he ducked behind a shrub and placed a finger to his earpiece. "Ready, Al."

"Copy. Three . . . two . . . one." A muffled, zapping sound filled the air for an instant, then died off. "Power out."

If it hadn't been for the dim light bleeding through a second-story curtain and the humming AC unit, Jason wouldn't have known if it worked or not. He waited in the silent aftermath of the power loss, expecting someone to be alerted and to search the property, but there was only silence and still no sign of life inside or around the house.

With the power secured and Jason no longer worrying about triggering a security system, he darted stealthily across the grass and climbed up to the eave under the second-story window. He took one more look around, then jammed his elbow against the glass with just enough force to shatter the square. Jason waited and listened, making sure no one was startled by the shattered glass. When all sounded clear, he reached inside and felt around until he gripped the locking mechanism.

Quietly, he slid the window aside just far enough for him to fit through, then unholstered his .45-caliber handgun and climbed inside. The bedroom was cool and nearly pitch black, with a neatly made king-sized bed, and a nightstand and dresser.

Keeping his Glock raised, he crept across the room and out into a hall, passing another empty bedroom before coming to a dining room with large windows that looked out over the dark water below. Like the bedrooms, the place looked untouched, like a hotel room when you first check in. There were no bags or signs of recent activity anywhere.

Jason checked downstairs and found a living room with a pool table, couches, and a small back bedroom. Seeing no sign of anyone being home, he reached for his earpiece to update the others. "There's nothing here."

"What do you mean, nothing?" Scott replied, his voice riddled with confusion.

"I mean, it's empty. Nobody's home. There's nothing in here except furniture."

Silence fell over the line.

What am I missing here? Jason thought, shaking his head as he scoured the living room again.

"What about the boat?" Alejandra chimed in. "Maybe there's a clue there."

"Yeah, maybe they've got more of those torpedoes stashed away," Finn added. "If we can figure out who their supplier is, maybe we can track down a client list."

Jason sighed, then headed back upstairs and took one final look around. Still not seeing anything out of place, he returned downstairs and toward the back door that led to the dock. Just as he gripped the knob, a thin layer of dirt on the tile floor caught his eye. He knelt down and brushed aside the nearby curtains, allowing moonlight to bleed inside.

"Footprints," he whispered as he investigated the markings.

He followed the prints, the tiny patches of dirt fading with every step as they led across the living room. But the steps quickly vanished just before reaching the back wall. He flicked on his flashlight for a better look, keeping it on its dimmest setting just in case they'd missed someone on the property. He'd expected to find the prints heading for the stairs or the door to the back room, but they didn't. They vanished in an instant.

Jason assessed the wall that was mostly covered by a beautiful watercolor painting of Saba. Rising back to his feet, he pressed an ear to the painting, rapped his knuckles against the canvas, and then the wall next to it. The space sounded hollow behind the canvas—a clear difference in acoustics.

Jason smiled. "Wait a second, guys," he said into the radio. "I think I found something."

Tapping his knuckles against the painting one more time, and fixating on the footprints by his feet, he was confident that he'd found a secret entryway.

The question is, how do I open it?

He ran his fingers around the entire frame, hoping to find a hidden mechanism that would cause the painting to slide out of place. When he came up empty, he pressed against the side, seeing if it would give, but the painting was locked in place and wouldn't budge.

"Try the pool cues," Scott said in his ear.

Jason forgot he was wearing a body cam and that everything he was doing was being watched and recorded in the command room of the *Valiant*. At first, he was against the idea, but after what Finn had caught on his camera earlier that day, and after some convincing on Scott's part, he'd agreed. He figured that maybe Scott could catch something that he missed.

Turning his attention to the rack of waxed narrow poles, Jason inspected them suspiciously.

"The one in the middle looks strange, don't you think?" Scott said.

Peering closer, Jason saw that the middle of the five cues was shorter and rested deeper in the stand. "Very observant," he said.

"See if you can pull it down," Scott said.

Jason pulled the polished wood, and the stick angled downward but didn't come loose. A mechanical click filled the air, followed by the hum of the painting rising to the ceiling and revealing a hollowed-out walkway behind it.

As if reading Jason's mind, Scott said, "When you've played pool with as many powerful men as I have, you learn a few tricks of the privacy trade."

Jason grabbed his pistol and held it up while creeping toward the opening. It was pitch black, so he aimed his flashlight and realized that it was a passageway that bore straight into the rock. "Now, this is more like it," he said. "You seeing this, Scottie?"

"Clear, Jase. That door must be running on backup batteries. Watch out for an alarm."

Jason kept the beam of light forward while stepping into the passageway. The narrow space opened up, revealing a room with a metal table, desk, and chairs. On the table was a chart of Anegada, with markings that Jason realized indicated parts of the reef that had been blasted away or that they were planning on blowing up.

Scanning the room, he found it hard to believe that the place had been built in the past few months. He imagined that the location had been used to hide illegal activities of one variety or another for years.

After poring over the room, Jason's eyes settled on a laptop resting on the desk. Cracking it open and seeing that it was password protected, he focused back on the chart pinned down to the table. He carefully examined the markings around Anegada, noticing that the blasts formed the beginnings of a distinct trail that dotted along the reef, just off the southwestern shore of the island.

"These blast sites sure as hell don't look random," he said into the radio. "It looks like they've been chosen for a reason. Almost like they're looking for—"

Suddenly, Alejandra's voice blared through his headset. "Jase! You've got two vehicles incoming. They just drove through the gate, and they're moving fast."

TEN

MOVING QUICKLY BUT methodically, Jason snatched the laptop and stowed it in his backpack. He'd already recorded everything inside and was confident they'd find more intel on the computer.

He made sure everything was as it was when he'd arrived, then hustled out of the hidden room. Once back into the living room, he pushed the middle pool cue back into place, and the painting slid back down over the opening. Darting for the back door, Jason switched off his flashlight and peeked out through the glass just as three shadowy figures appeared. The men stomped along the narrow porch, heading straight for the door.

You weren't kidding about them closing in fast, Al, he thought, cursing under his breath.

With his Glock still holstered, Jason wanted to engage the three—to beat and shoot his way to some answers, but the plan was reconnaissance only. Their covert group still didn't know who they were dealing with, what the criminals were up to, or how deep the operation went. Jason and his team were after the top brass—the ones with their fingers on the trigger. If a fight broke out, word would spread through the operation like wildfire. They wanted to learn what they could while staying under the radar, then pounce when their enemies least expected it.

"There's three more in the second SUV," Alejandra said. "Both vehicles are parked and still running."

Jason didn't have time to think through the situation. The men would reach the door at any second, so he needed to move. He needed to hide.

Dropping down and spinning on his heels, Jason ducked behind the couch and slid under the pool table just as the back door opened. The three men barged inside, single file.

"What the hell's wrong with the power?" the second man through the door barked in a strong Russian accent while flicking a light switch back and forth.

The glowing moonlight allowed Jason to see that they were all serious, tough-looking guys, but the bald man who spoke was the most imposing of the bunch.

"It's a Caribbean island," one of the other guys said as he shut the door behind them. "Power goes out all the time."

The leader seemed unconvinced. It was clear to Jason, right away, that the guy possessed experience beyond his comrades, that he was used to life-or-death situations, and that he'd developed a powerful sixth sense that could sniff out potential danger.

The bald leader stomped across the room, heading straight for the rack of pool cues set into the wall. He jerked the middle one down, and the painting lifted. "You heard what the big boss said," the man snarled, pointing into the dark secret space. "Load up everything. We're leaving."

The shortest of the group broke for the hidden passageway while the other rubbed the back of his neck as he approached the leader.

"It doesn't make sense for us to leave," a lanky man with slicked-back hair said. "We're so close."

"Orders are orders. Besides, we'll be back soon and better prepared for the next go-round."

The hulking bald man strode over to the pool table, his boots just inches away from Jason. Thankfully, the shadows kept him concealed, and he remained perfectly silent as the conversation continued.

"Time is not exactly on our side," the skinny guy said. "We need to strike while this iron's hot. Get in, and get what we came for before more people catch on to our activity. Like that guy earlier today."

The big man growled. "That nobody got lucky. And I easily got away from him. He never even got a good look at me with the gear on."

"Still, we should—"

Skinny was interrupted by a swift hand clutching his neck. The leader squeezed tight, wrestling the guy backward and slamming him against the pool table. Jason kept still as the wood creaked and groaned, hoping that the legs had enough strength to keep the table standing.

"You don't get paid to question your superiors. We're in charge, and if you don't like the way the boss or I do things, then we'll be happy to dispose of you and replace you with someone more suited to the task."

The subordinate gagged as his head was shoved harder into the felt and his feet hovered above the floor. His cellphone slipped from his front pocket, tumbling off the edge of the rail and rattling to the floor beside Jason.

With one hand still clutching Skinny's neck, the leader snatched the solid maroon billiard ball from a middle pocket with his other. "You question me again, and I'll bash a crater into your skull," he said, holding the dense orb up to the man's terrified eyes.

When Skinny nodded that he'd received the message, the leader casually dropped the ball onto the table.

"The laptop's missing!" the short man shouted from the entrance into the secret room.

The leader loosened his grip. "What?"

"It was on the table when we left, and now it's—"

The leader let go of Skinny's neck and hustled over to the room. Seeing for himself that the laptop wasn't on the table, he fumed with rage. "I knew something was . . . Search the grounds!" He snatched a radio from his hip and called in to the guys still in the SUV.

The guy who'd been manhandled onto the table rubbed his throat, still catching his breath from the violent lesson. The leader and the short guy grabbed their pistols and flicked on flashlights while heading for the stairs.

"You look down here," the leader shouted.

Skinny grabbed his weapon, turned on his light as well, then felt his empty pocket and remembered that his phone had fallen free. He peered over the green tabletop, then shifted his body and searched around for a split second before resting his eyes on the smartphone.

He coughed and knelt down, reaching for the device. As the guy gripped his phone, he paused as the beam from his flashlight shined under the table. The skinny man gasped, and his eyes sprang wide as he realized he wasn't alone. "Who the—"

Jason didn't let him finish. With no choice but to engage, he pounced from his hiding place, grabbing a fistful of Skinny's shirt collar. He bashed the guy's jaw into the edge of the table, then forced an arm around his neck and dragged him into the shadows. The man tried desperately to breathe and break free, but Jason flexed even tighter. After less than ten seconds of shaking, his body went motionless in Jason's arms.

Jason left him in the darkness and grabbed his backpack. Just as he crept around the table, he heard footsteps coming from the stairs.

As the short guy appeared and swept his pistol and the beam of his flashlight across the room, Jason grabbed the closest pool cue from the wall rack beside him. Gripping it tightly, he lunged forward and thrust the tip into the guy's throat. The chalk-covered end bore through the tender flesh just as he aimed his weapon at Jason. Having put all his weight and strength behind it, Jason impaled the cue through his neck, striking the wall behind him. The criminal let out a weak cry, his head snapping forward and his eyes bulging. He involuntarily relinquished his weapon, and his body lurched backward, collapsing over an end table.

Jason released the cue, and the moment the short man's body settled, movement and voices caught his attention just outside the window. It was the faint glisten of metal in the moonlight as a weapon was raised.

Jason turned and focused his gaze. His instinct taking over, he threw himself to the floor just as two men opened fire. Deafening pops of gunpowder filled the air, and rounds burst through the glass, soaring just over Jason's head and pelting the back wall. He rolled, snatched his Glock, then rose onto a knee, trying to get a look at his attackers. But the two men continued incessantly, firing round after round into the room and forcing Jason to stick to cover. With the staircase at his back, Jason knew that more criminals could close in on him from behind at any second.

"Jason, what's your status?" Scott said into the tiny radio that was still planted in Jason's left ear. "I can't see anything on the—"

"Pinned down!" he fired back, rolling again before rising to get an angle on his attackers.

The door slammed open, and one of the men appeared. He'd switched his handgun for a twelve gauge and pulled the trigger just as the door opened, sending a storm of pellets across the room. The projectiles tore the couch to shreds, nearly missing Jason as he rolled to the side of the room. As the guy cocked another shell into the chamber and discarded the empty, he shifted his aim. Jason knew he wouldn't get so lucky with the next shot.

He popped up just as his attacker was struck and jolted sideways, firing his second shell into the ceiling. Collapsing backward, the man rolled down the concrete steps, picking up speed before slamming into a metal railing. The second attacker tried to retaliate, but a bullet tore into his chest before he could take aim, sending him to the ground as well.

Alejandra appeared in the doorway, her Walther raised at chest height.

Striding inside and seeing the two men Jason had taken down, she said, "Still two left."

Jason jumped to his feet, bolted across the room, and grabbed his bag. The two headed for the stairs, ready to put the final nail in the coffin and finish off the remaining criminals. They raced up to the second level and, seeing it empty, continued up onto the roof. The moment the door opened, the sounds of a roaring engine filled the night air. They sprinted out and watched as one of the SUVs floored it away from the compound, heading for the main road.

"We got what we came for," Jason said, buckling the cross strap of his backpack. "We'll deal with those two another day."

Alejandra nodded, but as they turned to head down to the water and meet up with Finn, they both froze as they heard two muffled explosions coming from the house's foundation. The whole structure began to shake and angle forward toward the steep cliff face and the water far below.

ELEVEN

NEITHER JASON NOR Alejandra had time to think over what had happened. With the house shaking and angling over the edge of the cliff, they needed to move. Too high up to make a run and dive for the ocean, Jason gripped Alejandra by the forearm and motioned toward land.

"Come on!" he yelled, snatching the coil of rope and grappling hook from the side of his backpack.

The two took off in a mad dash, breaking as fast as they could. When they reached the edge of the roof, Jason scouted for an anchor point for the hook. With nothing in the driveway except for the idling suv, Jason reared back and hurled the grappling hook.

The rear window shattered, but the device failed to catch, bouncing free and swinging toward the side of the house.

"Running out of time, Jase!" Alejandra exclaimed as the house shook and angled farther forward.

Jason gathered the rope as fast as he could. Gripping the hook, he locked onto his target a second time, then launched the device through the air just as the house's foundation gave way. Jason and Alejandra were forced to hold onto the side of the house as the hook soared through the air, disappearing through the broken window of the SUV. This time, the arms sprang open and caught on the inside of the door.

With an arm wrapped around Alejandra, the two dove just as the house fell out from under them. The rope went taut, and they gripped each other as they swung from the chaos. Jason rotated, his back taking the brunt of the force as they collided with the newly cleared cliffside.

Gasping, the two looked back and watched as the entire house flipped forward off its blown-up foundation, breaking apart in a loud rumble as it fell down the steep slope and crashed into the Caribbean. The concrete house rapidly filled with water and sank into the dark abyss, leaving behind few remnants of its existence.

"Why are we moving?" Alejandra said.

Transfixed by the sight, Jason's mind shifted to their new predicament. They were slowly descending but picking up speed, and looking up, Jason realized that the vehicle they were anchored to had apparently been left in neutral.

"You've gotta be kidding me."

"There!" Alejandra said, pointing at a narrow ledge in the rock five feet beneath them.

With no other option aside from following the house to a watery grave over two hundred feet down, Jason lowered Alejandra and held her as they both swung back and forth. The SUV rolled backward faster, and swinging Alejandra with all his might, they both let go when she reached the top of her arc. The Latina flew through the air, her boots striking the ledge and her body planting flat against the rock face.

Jason saw the glowing-red rear lights of the SUV as it reached the edge. With no time left, he grabbed the rope, unhooked the carabiner, and hurled himself toward the rock. His boots missed the surface, and he was forced to catch the edge with his hands. He held on tight to the rock as the SUV rolled over the cliff, then soared through the air and whooshed right past them. The vehicle bashed against the sloping rock, tumbling like an empty soda can before crashing into the water. Like the house before it, the SUV filled with water and vanished into the sea.

After the chaos settled, Alejandra reached down and offered Jason a hand, helping to heave him up onto the ledge. "You know," she said, "as incredible as it is, I think that was our closest one yet."

He caught his breath while trying to wrap his head around the ordeal they'd just been through. The silhouette of Mount Scenery towered in the distance. "Now," Jason said, "all we need is for this volcano to erupt."

"Don't go jinxing it now."

The two crept along the ledge, then climbed up a gentler slope before plopping down onto a plateau and letting their adrenaline wear off. Since the house took most of the staircase with it when it avalanched into Davey Jones's Locker, they trekked around the side of the island for half a mile before reaching a steadier grade down to the water.

Finn appeared just as they reached the bottom, motoring the RHIB around a sharp point. "I'm gonna take a stab in the dark and say they found you, Jase," the Venezuelan said as they jumped aboard.

Jason removed his backpack and plopped down in the bow, resting his body against the pontoons. "What gave you that impression?"

"If the gunshots didn't do it, I'd say it was when that house decided to take an evening dip."

A radio crackled to life. "Come in for an update," Scott said. "Jason, Al, you two all right?"

"Never better, Scottie," Alejandra said.

"Nothing like a wild Wednesday night," Jason added into his earpiece as Finn piloted them away from the shoreline. "We took down four of them, but two got away. My guess is, they're heading for the airport."

"Nowhere else to go," Finn said. "Unless they've got another boat on the island."

"I've already communicated with ATCs over at Juancho," Scott said, referring to the only airstrip on the island.

Jason loosened the straps of his climbing harness. "You grounding them?"

"No, we're still playing catch up here. We need answers. We need to know where they're heading."

Jason gestured to the backpack on the deck between him and Alejandra. "Hopefully the laptop can help with that."

"Report back to the *Valiant*," Scott said. "It's time to crack open this operation and see what the hell these guys are up to."

TWELVE

SCOTT HAD A pot of coffee warm and ready for the trio when they entered the command room of the *Valiant*. They relished the warm, caffeinated drinks, needing the extra boost to keep their minds and bodies going after the long day they'd had.

Jason had a hard time believing that he and Finn had dropped beneath the waves and dove Horseshoe Reef earlier that day. He checked his watch and saw that the minute hand was just hitting midnight.

Between intermittent sips of coffee, the group discussed what had happened, then talked through options going forward.

"The muscular, bald leader of the group is the same guy that attacked us back at the reef," Jason said. "He mentioned his escape."

"He was one of the guys you took down?" Finn said.

Jason shook his head. "No, the leader made off in the SUV. Second time today he got away from me."

"Don't be so sure of that," Scott said. "Remember, you were wearing a bodycam, and we were able to get a good image of the guy's face when he threatened his buddy."

Finn shrugged. "How's that gonna help?"

Scott smiled confidently. "We've been experimenting more with facial recognition software. Murph says he should be able to figure out who it is, that is, if the guy has any records with a facial shot."

"It's comforting that all of our info is just a great hacker's whim away," Alejandra said.

"And then there's the private jet the two flew away on," Scott continued.

Jason nodded. "You're tracking it?"

Scott brought the GPS image up on one of the monitors. It showed a red dot inching slowly across open water. "It took off ten minutes ago, and it's heading across the Atlantic toward Europe."

"Europe?"

Finn chuckled. "Guess you two scared them off even more than we thought."

"They'll be back," Jason said. "I heard them chat about it. Their boss apparently called for them to fly off someplace, but it didn't sit well with one of the guys. One thing's for certain. Whatever motive they had for blowing up the reef, they're not done yet."

Scott motioned toward the criminal's laptop on the table. "Between the computer, the facial recognition, and tracking the private jet, we should be able to figure out who they are and what that motive is soon."

The three remained in the command room for half an hour longer, poring over research and going over potential theories. Finn suggested that if all else fails, they could use the minisub to dive down and take a look at the SUV and house wreckage.

Alejandra smiled and relaxed back into her chair. "You're always looking for an excuse to take that for a ride."

"You can't argue that it's a blast to pilot," Finn said. "And I like the idea of being the first one to explore Saba's newest dive site."

"Not a bad idea," Scott said. "There could be useful intel in that vehicle, but let's table it for now." The former SEAL commander checked his watch, then pinched the bridge of his nose. "It could be a while before Murph gets back to us." The screen still displayed the plane flying over the Atlantic. "And I'm sure it'll be at least five hours before that plane lands."

The group dispersed to their cabins to get some sleep. Jason, still wired and hungry from the exertion, raided the galley. He chowed down a salad and banana before crashing on his bed.

The following morning, they received a video call from Murph and assembled back in the command room. The notorious hacker appeared on the center monitor, his face covered by shadows in the dark room and a hood over his head. Their mysterious friend greeted them, his voice distorted to be low pitched.

"What did you find, Murph?" Scott said.

"I've been poring over online data for the past few days," he replied. "At first, I assumed they were just your run-of-the-mill poachers taking what they can illegally, then I dug deeper. With the new intel you've given regarding the advanced explosives, I'd agree that we have more sophisticated villains pulling the strings. And the image you sent me of baldy connected with an interesting match."

Jason raised his eyebrows. "Murph, you found him?"

He brought up a blurry image of a man in a suit walking out from a restaurant among a sea of others dressed just like him. A second picture came on the screen—a clear headshot of an angry, pale-faced man who was the spitting image of the guy Jason had chased.

"His name's Boris Konstantine," Murph said. "Formally of the Federal Security Service of the Russian Federation, the main successor to the KGB. He was part of the president's security service for seven years. Before that, he served in Spetsnaz, the Russian Special Forces."

Scott listened intently. "Any record of what he's been up to recently?"

"He has a record of being unnecessarily brutal in combat and as a security officer." Murph showed an image of a man whose face was beaten so badly that all they could see were purple bruises and black, swollen eyes. "He did this to a man he claimed went after the prime minister back in two thousand three. But no evidence was found that the guy Boris beat up was a hit man. He eventually died from this attack. Two years later, Boris was charged with criminal activity and thrown into Russia's high-security prison, the Black Dolphin, for three years. Since being released, his life has been even more in the dark, though he's apparently been working private-security gigs all over the place. In the past year, he's twice been linked to Nikolai Reznikov."

Jason gasped, then leaned back in his chair and gazed at the deck while resting his chin on a forefinger.

"Something significant about that name?" Finn said, seeing Scott react to it as well.

Scott cleared his throat. "He's a corrupt Russian oligarch, who, after squandering his inheritance, made a fortune by conning people on Wall Street."

"And he was also friends with my father," Jason said, turning his attention back to the group. "So, that should tell you all you need to know about the guy's character." He fell silent a moment, then added, "This whole operation reeks of his handiwork. Any theories on what they're up to, Murph?"

"Well, this is where it gets really juicy," the hacker said. "Reznikov recently returned from a safari in Africa. He was apparently in Tanzania around the same time as when a man named Julien Lestrange, who owned an impressive collection of historical artifacts, fell into a ravine and was eaten alive by a pack of hyenas."

"I'm guessing you don't think he slipped?" Alejandra said.

"I think it would be one hell of a coincidence."

Finn ran a hand through his hair. "So, why would this Reznikov guy murder some collector?"

"I'd say money had something to do with it," Alejandra said. "Like maybe Reznikov's after something the collector owned. But Scott, you mentioned that he's already rich, right?"

He shook his head. "He used to be. But there's good reason to believe he's having financial troubles. Mainly the fact that he's a con who's terrible with his money."

Jason leaned forward, concentrating on the monitor displaying the hooded hacker in the shadowy room. "You find anything out about this Lestrange guy?"

Murph folded his arms. "I learned that his collection is world-renowned, and that many of his most prized possessions are being auctioned off near his house in Venice on Saturday."

"How much do you wanna bet that this Reznikov guy is gonna pay a visit?" Alejandra said.

Finn rested a hand on the chart of Anegada displayed on the table. "But what does this have to do with underwater explosions in the Virgin Islands? Do you really think the two could be related?"

Scott nodded. "He's right. A man like Reznikov has to have dozens of illegal side hustles going on in various countries at any given time."

Jason exchanged glances with Scott, then rose to his feet. "Well, I can think of one way to find out."

THIRTEEN

VENICE ITALY
TWO DAYS LATER

NIKOLAI REZNIKOV SAT in a plush leather seat
at the stern of a classic wooden speedboat as it
motored through the Grand Canal. It was a warm,
clear evening, the last breaths of sunlight beaming
over the rooftops of the Queen of the Adriatic. They
motored past gondoliers leisurely rowing their traditional Venetian boats while wide-eyed tourists kicked
back and took in the sights. Dozens of delivery boats
chugged back and forth through the central waterway around them as they cruised under the famous
Rialto Bridge.

Just before the canal wrapped around San Marco, the pilot eased the shiny craft against the narrow promenade at the base of a beautiful three-story mansion.

"You and your men stay close, Boris," Reznikov said to the colossal bald man beside him.

When Boris nodded, Reznikov stood, flattened his dark blue suit, then stepped ashore. He tapped his ivory cane against the smooth stones as he strode into the shadow of the Palazzo Pisani Moretta. Reznikov barely regarded the exterior of the shining example of fifteenth-century Gothic architecture—the pink façade and mullioned windows with ogival arches.

After showing the host at the door his invitation, the Russian entered through one of the two central pointed arched doorways leading into the manor. In the palazzo's grand foyer, Reznikov passed by beautiful Baroque decorations that were the proud works of the best Venetian artists of the eighteenth century.

Following in the footsteps of generations of mankind's elite—including popes, presidents, and global celebrities—he sauntered to the second level via a double set of wide marble steps. Once at the top, Reznikov strolled through two massive double doors, entering the main hall and largest room of the house. He was greeted with idle chatter by a sea of men wearing suits and tuxedos and women in satin dresses and coated in diamonds.

Paintings covered the walls, and chandeliers hung from the ceiling and cast a warm light over the wide-open space. Rows of chairs covered half of the waxed floor, leading up to a temporary stage with a wide mahogany podium. Speakers were set up behind the stage, along with two large projector screens.

A thin man in a light blue suit stood beside the podium, checking his watch every thirty seconds as visitors admired the rows of items displayed in glass cases at his back.

Reznikov made his way through the group, greeting an occasional familiar face before settling into a chair in the front row. He didn't bother inspecting the collection. He already knew the item he wanted.

"Ladies and gentlemen," the man on stage said into a microphone. "We will be commencing the auction soon. Please make your way to your seats."

Once the group settled, filling nearly every seat in the hall, the auctioneer continued with a brief introduction about himself. He then expressed his thanks to the homeowners for providing the venue before speaking about the items they'd be bidding on that evening.

"Each of you has a rare opportunity to own a piece from one of the world's greatest private collections of historical artifacts," he said, his voice clear and powerful. "A collection that took the passionate Julien Lestrange half a century to assemble. We are proud to be able to fulfill his final wishes and auction off these items here today. As instructed in his will, all proceeds from tonight's transactions will be donated to various local and international charities."

The event's overseer cleared his throat and signaled for the first item to be brought forward. A short, older man behind him carefully set a glass case containing two old sketches onto the white-clothed table in front of the podium.

"We will begin with item number one, a pair of incredible pieces that date back to the fourteen forties. What you see here are original sketches done by Orban, the famous Hungarian engineer whose massive cannons were used by the Turks to batter down the walls of Constantinople. We will start the bidding at ten thousand euros."

Uninterested, Reznikov leafed through the brochure as bidding began, smirking as he passed over a picture of Lestrange posing beside his collection. He arrived at the lot schedule, and seeing that the item he was there to claim was deeper in the queue, strode to the bar and downed a few shots of Stoli.

The event continued for another hour and a half, and the bidding wars were broken up by occasional intermissions. Settling back into their seats, the group eyed the auctioneer as another item was brought up and placed onto the table before him. It was a small, old jug with faint faded markings covering its exterior. Unlike many of the shiny, elegant artifacts that were bid on that day, this item garnered little interest from the prospective bidders.

The auctioneer leaned forward and motioned toward the item. "I present item number twenty-four of today's lot. Though not as well-known or historically significant as most of the collection, this piece was one of Lestrange's most treasured, and it is believed to have belonged to William Kidd, the famous Scottish-born sailor who became one of the most renowned buccaneers of the Golden Age of Piracy." The man straightened his jacket and took a sip of water. "I will start the bidding at five-thousand euros."

An unenthusiastic hand raised a paddle into the air, starting off the bidding. A few paddles followed, and the bid rose to twelve thousand. As a quarter of the group broke away to use the restroom or get a drink, the bidding war dwindled to two people: an ample-bellied man in a white suit and a petite woman with short dark hair.

The two went back and forth, topping each other and bringing the bid up to eighteen thousand, a much greater sum than anyone had expected for the item. Claiming the highest bid with a confident paddle raise, the woman regarded the gentleman in white through a pair of black horn-rimmed glasses, hoping she'd conquered her foe.

The guy leaned back and chuckled, holding his hands out to the woman to let her know it was all hers. "I've got far too much junk already," he said, arousing a laugh from the group.

The woman bit her lip as she turned back forward and stared at the auctioneer in anticipation.

Even he let out a quick chuckle as he raised his gavel into the air. "Eighteen thousand going once . . . going twice . . ."

He was just about to signal an end to the round when Reznikov casually raised his paddle.

The auctioneer froze, then pointed the wooden mallet. "I've got nineteen thousand."

The woman shot a disappointed glance across the room.

Reznikov smirked. Relishing the look on her face, he whispered, "Not today, madam."

The woman leaned forward, adjusted her dress, and threw her paddle up again.

"Twenty thousand," the auctioneer said.

Reznikov grinned. He enjoyed messing with the woman, but it was time to end their little war. He raised his paddle. "Fifty thousand."

His bid was punctuated by gasps from the crowd. What was believed to have been an unnoteworthy artifact just received one of the highest bids of the night.

Reznikov observed the woman carefully, enjoying the sight of her squirming with anguish in her seat. She hunched forward, frowning and shaking her head.

"I have fifty thousand," the auctioneer said. "Going once . . . going twice . . . so—"

"Two million," a male voice said from the back of the room.

The auctioneer froze mid-word.

In a synchronized movement, every person in the room adjusted their position and turned to look back at who'd placed the staggering bid. The auctioneer was tongue-tied, taken aback by the enormous sum as a paddle sprouted up from the back of the hall.

Reznikov nearly choked on his drink when he turned, snarling as he leered toward the back of the room.

FOURTEEN

JASON CASUALLY LOWERED his paddle and peered toward the stage over the sea of people. In a fitted tux, Italian shoes, and with his dark hair slicked to the side, the tall, athletic American looked like two million euros as he swirled the ice in the old-fashioned. Every eye in the room stayed locked on him during the silent scene.

Reznikov's eyes bulged as he stared at Jason, trying to place where he recognized the young man from.

"I have two million from the gentleman in the back." The auctioneer paused, seemingly in disbelief at the sum he'd just uttered. "Going once . . . going twice . . ."

As he proclaimed "Sold!" and struck his gavel, Jason shifted his eyes to the Russian, shot him a confident smile, then raised his glass before taking a slow sip.

Reznikov growled and turned away as the auctioneer thanked Jason for the unparalleled act of generosity. Having conquered the Russian, and having fully enjoyed his reaction, Jason scanned the murmuring crowd of people staring his way, and then raised his drink toward the stage.

After wiping the sweat from his brow, the auctioneer continued with the next item.

"Two million?" Scott said into Jason's earpiece. "You don't think that was a little excessive?"

"It was more than worth it to see the look on that guy's face," Jason whispered back. "And hey, it's for a good cause, right? All for charity."

"Yeah, but we also like to keep a low profile. Or have you forgotten?"

Jason noticed Reznikov skirting around the edge of the rows of seats and approaching him. As he and the Russian locked eyes again, Jason turned away and said, "Regardless, I think that ship has sailed."

Jason lowered his hand and focused on the next item up for bid.

"Jason Wake," Reznikov said in his unmistakable, coarse Russian accent. "I couldn't believe my eyes for a moment. I must say, your presence is a surprise. And I see you're having no trouble spending your father's fortune."

"Well, I may never be on your level when it comes to exhausting a family fortune, Nik. I'm surprised to see you here, as well. I thought you'd be in New York searching for new ways to squeeze retirement dollars from hardworking citizens."

Reznikov chuckled at the slight. "No, no, boy. I've moved on to more lucrative ventures."

"You don't say? Well, I hope none of those lucrative ventures involve the jug I just nabbed."

"I didn't realize that you had such a keen interest in old kitchenware."

"No. Just winning. I guess I got something from my father, after all."

Reznikov gave a smug smile. "Well, if you're also like your father in that you crave female companionship, my long list of fresh beauties are at your disposal while you're here in Europe."

"If I ever become desperately lonely enough to require purchasing companionship, yours will be the first number I call. I need no reminder of your expertise in such matters."

The two stared at each other until the clicking of high heels on the floor caught their attention.

Alejandra appeared in a tight green dress and had her brown hair pulled back in a classy bun. Dazzling the group with her runway-model looks, she wrapped an arm around Jason. "The auction is about to resume."

The Russian ogled the beautiful Latina, making no attempt at discretion. "Nikolai Reznikov," he said, extending a hand to Alejandra.

She shook and gave only her first name.

He shot her a smile when he eventually let go. "It's a pleasure to meet you, Alejandra."

She replied only with a nod, then whispered into Jason's ear, "He's even scarier in person."

"Excuse me, Nik," Jason said, patting Reznikov on the shoulder, "but I have to get a refill before the next round of bidding starts." He held up his nearly empty old-fashioned. "Then I might sample the hors d'oeuvres. There's something about winning items at auction that works up the appetite, don't you agree?" The Russian narrowed his gaze, and Jason added, "You sticking around?"

Reznikov's face tightened for a moment, then he brushed off the brief lapse of composure. "No, no. It's time for me to leave, Mr. Wake. But I have a feeling our paths will cross again soon."

The Russian nodded to Alejandra and gave her a final predaceous smile before turning for the exit, his cane clacking against the sleek floor.

Her arm still wrapped under Jason's elbow, Alejandra escorted him along the back row of chairs, weaving through the fringes of the group. "Well, I just got my whole year's supply of passive aggression," she said.

The two strolled over to the bar, but Jason kept his eyes locked on Reznikov, watching as the Russian left through the open double doors.

"Hey," Alejandra said, tapping him on the shoulder. "You all right?"

As the Russian disappeared from view, Jason blinked, then noticed he was squeezing the handle of his bidding paddle so tightly that his fingers were pearly. He'd only met Reznikov twice before, and it had been years since those interactions, but he could remember feeling decisively uncomfortable around him, and those emotions had only amplified with age. Reznikov made Jason's blood boil, no matter how hard he tried to keep calm.

"Here, have some water," Alejandra said after the bartender placed a glass on the counter.

"I'll have a whiskey," he said. "Straight up."

The bartender whirled around to pour the drink, and Alejandra stared at Jason while pursing her lips.

"Who are you, and what have you done with Jason Wake? Besides the Painkiller on Anegada, I can't remember the last time you drank." She pointed toward the empty glass still in his left hand. "Even that old-fashioned is virgin."

"That Red Stripe in Haiti," Jason said.

"If that even counts."

The term *health freak* didn't do Jason justice. He rarely consumed anything that was considered even remotely unhealthy.

The bartender returned and set the drink down.

Jason dropped back the entire lowball glass. The amber liquid went down smooth, then burned like a fireball when it hit his stomach. He raised his empty glass to the bartender. "Thank you. That hit the spot."

The barman smiled and gave a quick bow before helping another patron.

"Don't worry," Alejandra said. "If he comes back, I'll prevent him from saying more mean things to you."

Jason chuckled. "The only thing you'll have to prevent is me bashing in his pale, wrinkly face."

The auctioneer's assistant approached Jason as they leaned against the corner of the bar.

"Mr. Wake," the assistant said. "I have your financial institution's information, but I need you to approve the transfer before you can claim the item. Usually, I'd handle this after the event, but given your expressed interest to take possession of the artifact right away, we require the payment up front."

Jason motioned for the worker to join him at the edge of the stage, then looked back at Alejandra.

"Don't worry about me," she said, shaking her hand in disgust that she'd touched the Russian criminal's hand. "I need to use the ladies' room to wash up anyway."

After transferring the funds, the assistant thanked Jason again for his generous contribution. A clerk brought over the artifact and began wrapping it in cloth. He was about to place it in a metal case when Jason waved him off.

"I don't need the case," he said.

The clerk looked up, stunned. "You're just gonna walk out of here carrying an item you paid two million for?"

Jason shrugged. "That's the plan."

Astonished, the assistant handed Jason the piece, then gave him a business card. "Please, if you ever wish to come to one of our events in the future, I'd be happy to have you as an honored guest."

Jason glanced across the hall toward the corridor Alejandra used to get to the restroom. Now that they had what they'd came for, he wanted to get out of there before Reznikov changed his mind about accepting the loss.

Alone with the item for the first time, Jason ran his fingers over its rough edges. The handle was missing, and the surface was so battered he was surprised that the old pottery was still holding together. He perused every inch of the container, but nothing caught his attention as peculiar or noteworthy. At the rim, the jug was so corroded and worn that the opening was nearly blocked, making it difficult to see inside, even under the glow of a nearby chandelier.

Now to figure out why Reznikov wanted you so badly, Jason thought. *And what connection you have to explosions off—*

"Congratulations on claiming the big-ticket item," a woman behind him said. "Your bid will be the talk of the town, I'm sure."

Jason turned around to see the woman who'd been caught in the artifact's bidding war prior to Jason crashing the party.

"I'm Charlotte Murchison," she said, holding out her hand.

He accepted it and replied, "Jason Wake."

She pursed her lips, then smiled and admired the item in Jason's hands. "I assume that, given the sum you've paid for it, you're aware of its historical significance and the legend surrounding it."

"Legend?"

She eyed Jason like he was crazy. "Of Kidd's lost treasure, of course. The treasure he alluded to when he was brought to trial before the admiralty."

"Oh, right," he said. "I've heard something about that."

He made a mental note to research the legend the woman was referring to, then resumed his search for Alejandra.

"So . . . are you going to look inside?"

"I'm pretty sure it's empty." Jason glanced at the bartender, who was whipping up another order. "But I'm sure you'd enjoy the drinks they serve here more. I mean, I'm all for vintage, but—"

"No, I mean the clue," she said, lowering her voice and looking around. "The clue that Kidd supposedly hid inside that container."

Jason held up the jug and inspected it again, trying to peek inside the narrow opening.

Charlotte placed a hand to his arm, then ushered him toward a corner, out of earshot from anyone else in the hall. "Few people know about it, let alone believe it could be true," she explained. "But Lestrange never let anyone near the thing to find out. He kept it hidden away in a secret safe for years." She stepped closer to Jason and lowered her voice even more. "I have a setup in place to examine it—a small camera we could use to figure out if there's any truth to the legend. I was planning to inspect it after I won the item but never thought it would go so high."

As Jason thought over her words, a group of men marched through the double doors and into the grand hall. The woman continued to talk, but Jason didn't process a word of what she said. His attention was fixed on the newcomers, and as they got closer, Jason recognized the leader of the group. Boris Konstantine, the Russian criminal killer he'd ran into twice in the Caribbean, zeroed in on Jason standing across the room.

FIFTEEN

"**M**R. WAKE," THE woman said, raising her voice. "I'm sorry, but are you listening to anything—"

Jason grabbed her by the shoulder. "You need to get out of here. Now!"

Her face paled, and her body went rigid.

Jason didn't have time to explain himself further or to think over his options. Boris was forcing his way through the group of people with two of his buddies right on his heels.

Spotting a side door to his right, Jason rushed for the alternate exit from the hall. As he reached for his earpiece to tell Alejandra it was time for them to get the hell out of there, a strong hand gripped his wrist from behind. Jason spun around as a tough man with a thick black beard tried to force him to the ground.

With his left hand still clutching the artifact, Jason stomped a heel down onto the guy's right foot, then ripped his hand free. The man growled and retaliated by slamming Jason down and pinning him to the counter. Jason nearly let go of the jug as he tried his best to fend the guy off, but when the bartender slid a highball glass down the counter, Jason caught the sparkling crystal, smashed it into the counter, then jammed the sharp, jagged edges into the guy's face. Shards of glass tore at his skin, and he yelled out while reaching for the wounds.

Given a brief window of opportunity, Jason pried open the space between them by forcing a leg up and driving his heel into the guy's chest, hurling him backward. He landed hard and rolled twice before colliding with the wall, his hands still grasping at the shards in his face as he yelled in pain.

Jason shot a quick thank-you look to the bartender, but as he focused back toward the center of the room, he realized that Boris and his henchmen had picked up their pace and nearly closed the gap.

Suddenly, a high-pitched alarm blared out, echoing across the room. The group of men froze, and the rest of the room pressed hands to their ears and whirled around in confusion.

The auctioneer scrambled to the podium. "Ladies and gentlemen, please make your way to the exit in an orderly fashion."

With everyone standing and funneling toward the door, the men were forced to fight their way against the current to continue across the room.

Alejandra popped into view from Jason's right. "This way!" she said, motioning toward the door at her back.

Jason sprang toward her, and the two dashed through the door and down a hallway.

"Can't I leave you alone for two minutes without you getting into trouble?" she said between breaths.

They sprinted to the back stairwell, planning to slip quietly out of the mansion, but froze as they heard men hustling up from the ground level.

A powerful, low-pitched voice yelled out, "Freeze, Wake!" Boris stormed into the hall, the two other men still right behind him. The lead Russian reached under his coat and gripped a pistol from his waistband.

The second Jason laid eyes on him, he and Alejandra booked it up the stairs, rounding the corner of the banisters as Boris opened fire. The gunfire shook the mansion to life like a barrage of lightning strikes, and people screamed even over the sounds of the fire alarm in the main hall.

"They got guns past the security," Jason said as they rounded another corner and raced up the final set of steps. "Of course they got guns past security."

"Suffice to say, you've really pissed this guy off, Jase."

The two cut a sharp left, then shouldered into a bedroom. Running across the space, they pushed through another door and locked it shut behind them. The mansion's website provided blueprints of the structure, which they'd studied meticulously during the flight across the Atlantic. They entered the library that had curtained windows overlooking both the Grand Canal on one side and distant rooftops on the other.

The two brushed aside one of the thick purple curtains and opened a window. As images of the structure and its blueprints had shown, there was a narrow walkway and a built-in ladder leading up to the roof.

Alejandra hopped out first. As she grabbed hold of the bottom rungs and began to climb, a man kicked open the closest door and stormed into the room. Wanting to take the guy down before he opened fire, Jason rammed the base of a vintage chaise lounge with his right foot, and the heavy piece of furniture slid across the wooden floor, striking the guy in the knees.

He lost balance, and by the time he caught himself, Jason had already closed the distance. He knocked the guy's pistol free, then grabbed the edge of the open door and slammed it into his head. Dazed, the guy retaliated with a desperate punch to Jason's rib cage, knocking the air from his lungs.

As his adversary geared up for another strike, Jason bashed his forehead into the guy's nose, breaking the fragile bones. When he yelled and lurched back, Jason spun and kicked him with a powerful roundhouse, knocking him off his feet and launching him back through the doorway.

"Jase!" Alejandra yelled through the open window.

Jason turned as Boris burst through the middle door into the library. Rolling behind the chair he'd kicked, Jason scrambled for the first guy's pistol and took cover as the Russian opened fire, sending a series of rounds that tore up the couch and rattled the air. Jason took aim under the couch, hoping the catch his attacker off guard and send a round into his foot, but the dexterous criminal already moved.

Boris momentarily ceased firing, allowing Jason to hear his heavy footsteps closing in. Just as Jason popped up, he was welcomed by the angry man charging at full speed. Boris snarled and dove, throwing his shoulder into Jason's chest and tackling him to the ground. Jason kept a tight grip on the jug, but the hefty blow caused the old artifact to smash to pieces beside them.

The big man didn't let up. Just as they smacked against the floor, he pounded Jason with two quick punches. He was strong and well trained, and he had the upper hand. Needing to do something to even the odds, Jason ignored the pain as he struggled for position and looked for anything he could use as a weapon.

"It's over, Wake!" Boris snarled. "You never should've meddled in our affairs. You're soft. You're no match for a warrior from Mother Russia!"

Reaching behind his head, Jason gripped the closest clay shard from the broken jug and stabbed it into Boris's left cheek. Surprised and in intense pain from the blow, Boris roared and pressed a hand to his bleeding face.

Jason jerked back the clay that was dripping with blood, then kicked the brute off of him. "You were saying, Boris?"

As he fumbled to his feet, Jason noticed something etched into the shard. Focusing closer, he realized that it was a series of seven numbers: 6141664.

The moment his brain processed what he was looking at, he heard a yell, followed by Boris storming toward him like a runaway freight train. Jason geared up for round two, but the enraged criminal caught him off guard with a leg sweep, followed by a one-two combo that ended with him throwing Jason through one of the front-facing windows.

The shard fell from Jason's hand as he crashed through the glass and was consumed by blurry chaos as he flew out into the evening air.

SIXTEEN

ALEJANDRA HELD ON tight to the rungs of the ladder, watching as the injured criminal tossed Jason through the window. His body quickly vanished, and Boris barely held on behind him, catching himself on the window jambs before flying out as well. The sound of shattering glass was soon punctuated by a distant splash in the Grand Canal.

Alejandra couldn't see where Jason hit the water. All she knew was that he'd just been struck multiple times, then freefell over forty feet to the water below. She watched as the Russian criminal stabilized himself and turned around.

"He's in the water!" Boris shouted at his posse as they flooded into the library.

Severely outnumbered, Alejandra had no chance of taking all of them down on her own, especially since she was unarmed. And even if she could reach the shattered artifact in time, she'd never get out of there with all of the pieces. She had only one option: to run.

As she adjusted her body on the ladder, her foot slipped on the bottom rung. Though barely able to catch herself, the act caught the attention of Boris and his comrades.

"Stop her!" the Russian yelled, stabbing a finger toward Alejandra as he stomped across the room.

Throwing stealth to the wind, Alejandra threw herself up the ladder as fast as she could, then climbed over the edge of the roof just as Boris leaned his head out the window.

"You two go and get her!" she heard Boris yell. "The rest of us on Wake. And call in the backup—"

The man's barking orders drifted away in the distance as Alejandra rushed to the top of the pointed clay-tiled roof. With the sun recently dipping beneath the horizon, leaving the Floating City in an ever-growing darkness, Alejandra peeked over the front edge, hoping to catch a glimpse of Jason. But all she saw was a tiny cluster of bubbles on the surface, along with passersby on the shore and people on boats pointing at the water where he'd vanished.

Alejandra didn't have time to make sure Jason was all right. Startled by the sounds of approaching men, she threw off her high heels and booked it barefoot across the rooftop. She used the slope of the opposite side of the roof to keep out of their view, then cut behind a dormer before sliding toward the backside of the mansion.

Easily traversing the gap to an adjoining roof, she picked up her pace, trying to lose the thugs chasing after her. She jolted and zagged to the right as her pursuers fired, sending bullets whizzing past her and pelting the shingles. Keeping her eyes focused forward, she realized that she was about to run out of horizontal surfaces. The roof ended, giving way to a bustling street far below. To her right was a canal, and to her left was a wide-open courtyard three stories down.

With her attackers opening fire again, she had no choice but to take on the gap. She picked up her speed, pumping her arms and pushing off the tiles as hard as she could. Aiming for a second-story rooftop on the other side of the street, she drove her right foot into the edge and hurled herself through the air. Soaring over ten feet, she barely conquered the void, landing hard on the other side and breaking off pieces of clay. She rolled across the roof and did everything she could to slow herself before tumbling over an eave and crashing into a rooftop garden.

As she shifted her battered body and struggled out of a sea of rosemary branches, a short, hunched-over woman in her eighties yelled at her in Italian while waving a pair of pruning shears. Alejandra didn't speak Italian well, but she knew the woman was angry as hell.

Alejandra shimmied out of the branches and planted her feet just as she heard pounding against the rooftop overhead. One of the guys had followed her, clearing the gap right on her heels. Wanting to stay hidden, Alejandra stared wide-eyed at the hysteric woman, placing a finger to her lips to try to keep her quiet. But the act only angered the Venetian more, and she raised her voice louder while pointing the tips of her shears at Alejandra.

The criminal ran toward the commotion, quickly reaching the corner of the roof. He wasted no time engaging, leaping from the shingles and landing smoothly right beside the woman. The local was shocked silent for a moment, then resumed her barrage, turning her attention to the man and aiming her shears at him.

Giving a smug smile, he pushed aside the woman, then lunged toward Alejandra. The Latina rushed toward the criminal, and at the last second, swiped her right leg, striking the man's shins and flipping him forward. Before the stumbling guy could reach for his pistol, Alejandra gripped a nearby shovel and bashed it across his face. His head snapped sideways, and drool spewed from his mouth as he collapsed into a plot of dirt.

Alejandra turned as the second criminal landed against the roof and rushed toward her. The Italian woman had regained her balance and resumed her tirade, waving the pruning shears at Alejandra. Knowing that trying to reason with her was futile, Alejandra lunged toward the woman and swiftly relieved her of her shears. Hearing the trailing guy approach, she ran to the wall, climbed up the uneven surface, then gripped the corner of the eave with her left hand.

Just as the guy appeared, she stabbed the shears into his right calf. The criminal shrieked, and his legs buckled. He keeled over, his body flipping before landing face-first onto the hard floor. Alejandra dropped back to the terrace and finished off the squirming, groaning criminal with a kick to the side of his head.

The Italian woman's mouth was locked wide open as she looked from both bodies and up to Alejandra.

After grabbing a guy's pistol, Alejandra handed the stunned woman back her shears, apologized for the mess, then hustled across the garden and climbed onto an adjoining rooftop. With her heart pounding, she reached the other side of a house, looked around, then plopped down to catch her breath.

"Note to self," she said, inspecting the dirty, cut-up bottoms of her feet. "Never wear a dress and heels again."

Having lost her radio during one of her many hard landings, she looked around to try and get her bearings. Hearing boat engines getting louder, she leaned over the side of the structure and watched as a white speedboat motored into view, followed by a fancy wooden craft chugging less than two hundred yards behind it. She concentrated on the lead boat and realized Finn was piloting it.

But where's Jase? she thought, scanning the waterway.

Shouts to her left alerted her to a man running onto a bridge with an assault rifle and staring at Finn as the Venezuelan piloted toward him. Tourists and locals fled the scene, getting clear of the gunman as he raised his weapon toward the canal.

Alejandra propped herself onto one knee, gripped her pistol with two hands, and took aim.

SEVENTEEN

JASON SPUN WILDLY, freefalling among a storm of glass toward the canal. He did everything he could to straighten his body and control his landing, and he just managed to sweep his feet beneath him before splashing into the water. The dark canal swallowed him whole, and he torpedoed fifteen feet down before coming to a stop in the dark, bubbly vortex.

He fought to get his bearings, maintaining his depth as he swam up to the base of the promenade. Barely able to see his hand in front of his face, he felt his way along the house's old foundation and covered thirty yards in the murky canal before reaching the corner of the mansion. With his lungs throbbing, he kicked as hard as he could, swimming out of the Grand Canal and into the Rio di San Polo. His heart pounding with adrenaline and quickly using up precious oxygen, Jason had no choice but to surface.

He kept to the wall, poking his head up for a quick lungful of air and a peek around the walkway before vanishing back into the channel. He didn't see anyone, but he did hear a guy yelling from up in the palazzo, informing his comrades that Jason was in the water.

When he popped up for air a second time, nearly out of sight of the house around a bend, he reached for his radio, hoping it hadn't been damaged by the confrontation. After seeing that it was still working, he pressed the talk button.

"Where you at, Finn?"

After a few seconds, Finn replied, "Heading your way. How's the water?"

"Let's just say there's a reason Venetians don't allow people to take a dip." He took a whiff of the water, then scrunched his face. "And it isn't to rain on the tourists' parade."

Jason kept his body pressed against the stone edge of the canal with only his head above water. Gazing in the direction he'd come, he watched as a white, eighteen-foot bowrider motored toward him. He let out a sigh of relief when he saw his short Venezuelan friend manning the helm.

Finn slowed as he approached, both keeping their eyes peeled for more of Reznikov's goons. After swimming to the port gunwale, Jason gripped the railing and heaved himself up out of the canal, plopping onto the deck beside the console.

"Jeez, you weren't kidding," Finn said, wafting a hand in front of his nose.

Jason scanned over the deck, then gestured back toward the mansion. "Any sign of Alejandra?"

Finn shook his head, then looked Jason over. "Where's the artifact? I thought you . . ."

Jason brushed the hair from his forehead. "Long story, but I'll tell you all about it when—"

The sound of an engine roared toward them. Jason peered over the stern just as a wooden speedboat appeared. Two men stood in the cockpit, both staring straight at him and Finn.

"Punch it, Finn!" Jason shouted, grabbing hold of the rail.

Finn peeked over his shoulder, locked eyes on the rapidly approaching boat, then shoved the throttle forward. They held on tight as the forty-horsepower outboard whined, accelerating the propeller full speed and jolting the craft forward. The bow tilted up as the boat rapidly climbed up on plane, rocketing through the quiet canal.

While Finn maneuvered them through the water-way, Jason peeked back as their pursuers kept up with them.

"Looks like we've got more company up ahead, Jase!"

Jason turned around and watched as a guy ran along a bridge just ahead of them. He took post in the middle, gripping a submachine gun in his hands.

Jason shook his head. "Crap, how many guys did this man send?"

"After what we did to them in Saba, and after your blow to his ego, I'm guessing his whole damn entou-rage!"

Jason did his best to stabilize himself on the bow, but a sharp turn to avoid the arrival of a delivery boat from an adjoining waterway threw off his balance. By the time he regained it, the guy on the bridge was already taking aim straight toward them. As Jason kept down and tried to think of a plan, a loud crack cut across the air. His heart pounded, and he was sure a bullet would strike his chest. Instead, he watched as the armed criminal on the bridge fell backward, dis-appearing from view.

Moments later, their guardian angel appeared in the form of Alejandra striding onto the bridge, pistol in hand. Finn slowed as he cut under the walkway, allowing Alejandra to climb over the railing and leap down onto the padded bow. Jason helped control her landing, and just as they were secure, Finn shoved the throttles forward again.

He rapidly brought them back up to speed, but slowing down allowed their attackers to close the gap even more. As Finn weaved them in and out of passing boats, Alejandra staggered to the stern and took cover while aiming over the thundering engine. She fired off shots at the approaching boat, shattering the windscreen with one of the rounds and prompting both men to drop back.

Onlookers pointed and gasped from boats and the flanking walkways.

Wind slapped at their faces as Jason dropped down beside Alejandra. "How many rounds you got left, Al?"

With the two men taking cover, she swiftly removed the magazine, checked the cartridge windows, then shoved it back into place. "Four."

"Hold on!" Finn said as he avoided a gondola that had just arrived from another canal. The pilot standing on the bow of the local craft dug his oar into the water, doing his best to avoid Finn's speeding boat, but it clipped the wooden bow, sending him and the couple sitting at the stern flying into the water.

As they rounded another bend, Jason slid down beside Finn. "We can't outgun them. You have to get them off our tail somehow."

"Venice is the perfect place to lose someone on the water," Alejandra said.

Finn maneuvered around another cluster of small boats. "Or to get lost."

"I thought you brought a map."

"You ever look at a map of Venice? The city's like the world's largest maze."

Loud pops erupted at their backs, along with Alejandra's voice telling them to get down. One of their pursuers had summoned the courage to rise back up and open fire, but his shots were sporadic, splashing into the canal and pelting the old walls as Finn zigged and zagged toward what appeared to be a dead end up ahead. The canal was supposed to continue through the bustling Santa Croce district, but there was construction underway, and a barge blocked the channel.

Maintaining their speed, Finn turned to the left, spraying water over the walkway as they roared into the Rio Marin. Alejandra fired two more times, trying to keep their pursuers down as Finn piloted them around a long turn, putting the other side of the winding Grand Canal in their sights.

Just as they were about to reach the opening out of the small channel, a long rubbish-collecting boat cruised right in front of them. Finn eased back and cut around them, but the hull struck the right side of the promenade, nearly spinning them out of control.

When they reached the Grand Canal, their pursuers were still a hundred yards behind them, and Alejandra was down to her last two rounds. Finn kept his attention forward, looking for any way out of the mess. Near a sharp turn in the channel up ahead, he focused on a construction site with a floating platform rising just a few inches from the water. Finn also spotted a large ferry heading toward the site and chugging parallel to the shore.

With time and bullets running out, Finn turned sharply and kept her full speed as he cruised along the shoreline. With their pursuers making a wider turn, they kept to the middle of the channel while taking ground and preparing to aim.

Finn gunned it, then cut a hard right, nearly flipping the craft before easing the speed down on the left side of the ferry. As Finn had hoped, their pursuers turned right away, flying along the right side of the ferry to try and cut them off. But instead of continuing forward, Finn hit full reverse, and the engine protested as the craft jerked back. Not wanting to be flooded by their own wake, Finn spun the wheel to the left, then slid the throttle forward again, rocketing them away from the ferry and heading south into the Rio Novo.

Jason, Finn, and Alejandra looked back just as their pursuers appeared, racing around the bow of the ferry but unaware of the flat construction barge laden with piles of dirt. The pilot tried desperately to avoid the collision, turning the wheel as sharply as he could, but their boat was moving too fast, and they smashed into the barge. The craft jerked out of the water, and its momentum drove the hull into a mound of dirt before flipping and breaking apart. The two men were barely able to let out cries of terror before they vanished in the chaos of the wreckage.

EIGHTEEN

WITH THEIR TAIL taken care of, Finn maneuvered them through the heart of the Dorsoduro District, around the Punta Della Dogana, and east to their hotel on the waterfront. They motored past the crowded rows of docks, up a channel, and stopped right beside the entrance to the Hotel Danieli.

Finn killed the engine, and they hopped out.

"Do us a favor and keep her covered," Jason said, handing the valet a twenty-euro note as the man welcomed them back and climbed aboard.

He scanned Jason's drenched body, then froze when he saw the bullet holes in the back of the boat. "Is everything all right, signor? Do you need the authorities?"

"Just a cover for the boat, thanks."

The valet nodded, fired up the engine, and cruised the boat back out of the channel, easing it into a row of dozens of other moored crafts.

The trio strode into the luxury hotel and to their two-bedroom suite. After a much-needed shower and change, they headed to the rooftop restaurant for dinner.

Featuring a spread of candlelit tables and various potted plants, the perch offered breathtaking views and an inviting ambiance on the warm summer evening. The hostess set them up with a table near the corner overlooking the busy, dark waters of the San Marco Basin. Across the other side of the rooftop, they saw the bright glow of city lights. A pianist's performance resonated from inside, a chorus of city chatter and activity in the background.

They relaxed into their seats, then placed their orders.

"I still can't believe we went through all that trouble and have nothing to show for it," Finn said after the waiter left.

"Maybe, maybe not," Jason said. He pulled a slip of paper from his pocket, unfolded it, and placed it on the white tablecloth.

Alejandra and Finn leaned over the table, trying to get a good look at the numbers written on the paper.

"I was wondering what you were scribbling after we entered the room," Alejandra said.

Finn inspected it closer. "Seven random numbers. Am I missing something here?"

Jason took a sip of water. "Those numbers were written on the inside of the jug."

"The jug that you won and then destroyed?" Finn said.

"I've been running them through my mind ever since I saw them."

"Six one four, one six six four," Alejandra said. "Any idea what they mean?"

"Not at all. A date, maybe? But if we can figure that out, we might be able to discover where Reznikov and his goons will go next."

Alejandra rested her chin on her fist. "That is, if they also figure it out."

"They got the whole pile, remember?" Jason said. "If there's more to it than just these numbers, that means they've already got a serious leg up on us when it comes to finding the treasure."

Both Alejandra and Finn froze.

"Treasure?" Alejandra said.

Jason told them about the discussion he'd had with the woman back at the auction—about how Captain

Kidd had supposedly hidden away his treasure trove and left a clue to its whereabouts long before his day at the gallows.

The waiter returned with their food, and they eagerly chowed down on the assortment of sirloin, turbot filets, and gnocchi, along with fresh salads and ginger and lemongrass soup.

Finn swallowed a bite, then washed it down with water. "So, this guy Reznikov wanted that old jug because it could lead to some pirate treasure? Doesn't that seem a little far-fetched?"

"More than a little," Jason said. "But it explains why Reznikov wanted it so badly."

Alejandra nodded. "And why his men have been blowing up the reef off Anegada."

As they continued to discuss possible theories and where they should go next, Jason gazed out over the moonlit waters of the basin and the distant Adriatic beyond. The night was calm, and the air had cooled significantly. To the west, he could see the famous Doge's Palace and the Basilica di Santa Maria beyond.

Venice was a sight to behold during the day, but at night, all lit up and bustling with life, she was like a vibrant, intoxicating dream. A poem come to life. Music filled the air, along with the smells of basil and sage mixed with the fresh sea breeze. Boats of all shapes and sizes came and went, blending into the canals of the city.

As Jason let his thoughts wander, hoping to find some solution in the deep confines of his mind, he recognized someone strolling west along the waterfront. "I'll be right back," he said, pushing back his chair.

Alejandra turned, fixing her attention toward the waterfront. "You see someone?"

"Jeez, don't tell me," Finn said. "Can't these guys give it a rest, at least until we finish eating?"

"It's not one of Reznikov's thugs," Jason said, still staring at the passing figure while polishing off his water. "It's the woman I told you about."

He weaved toward the elevator, burst out the doors at the ground floor, and rushed through the lobby and onto the boardwalk. Hustling down the promenade, he swept the area when he reached the corner at the bank of the Rio del Palazzo.

Jason caught a glimpse of the woman as she passed by St. Mark's column, entering the plaza bearing the same name on the other side of the waterway. Jason took off, meshing through the crowd, cutting across the historic Ponte della Paglia bridge, and rushing into the plaza.

Considered one of the finest squares on Earth, and Venice's prime attraction, the massive stone-paved expanse is flanked by some of the most impressive structures ever built, including the famous Basilica. Jason blended into the square that was filled with lively Venetians, tourists, and flocks of pigeons. Covering over five acres, he had his work cut out for him as he kept his eyes peeled for the woman in the red dress.

He passed through the crowd of thousands of people eating outdoors or walking arm in arm while listening to local performers and admiring the artists' work and fountains sculpted hundreds of years ago.

Jason climbed onto a bench for a better view near the base of the Campanile, a three-hundred-foot reconstruction of the bell tower originally built in the twelfth century. Surveying the busy scene, he saw no sign of the woman. Even in the daytime, it would be hard to spot somebody in the square, but the dark made it nearly impossible.

Focusing on a cart loaded down with various souvenirs, he tilted forward and grinned as he watched the woman stride around a corner and into view, poring over items for sale. Jason hopped off the bench and cut the distance, dodging people before collecting himself and catching his breath on the opposite side of the souvenir cart.

He stepped around the corner with a smile on his face, ready to continue their previous conversation, but the woman was nowhere in sight, having seemingly vanished. Jason turned to the local to ask where the woman had gone, and as soon as he opened his mouth, she appeared from his back.

"Are you following me, Mr. Wake?" Charlotte said, her hands planted on her hips.

"No, I—"

"What the hell happened back there? You tell me to get out of the place, then you smash a guy's face with a glass, and a bunch of men chase you out of the room. Next thing I know, alarms are sounding and guns are going off, and everyone's running like mad for the exit. Tell me, was it all because of the item you won?"

When the gift shop salesman stepped between them and tried to entice Jason with a keychain, the American waved him off and ushered Charlotte away from the cart. "Yes," Jason said. "Those men were after the artifact."

"So, you *did* know about the legend." She shook her head. "I knew you must have. Why else would you have paid so much for such a piece?"

"No, I didn't. I was trying to . . ." He looked at the crowd surrounding him. Venice was a big city, and he knew that the chances of one of Reznikov's guys being close by was slim to none, but it still wasn't worth the risk. "We should talk somewhere more private."

"You think I'd go anywhere with you after what happened today?"

"Please, Charlotte. Just let me explain."

"Why? What do you need me for?"

"I need your help to figure out the clue."

The woman's eyes lit up. "So, there *is* a clue," she gasped. "The legend is—"

"Yes," Jason said, watching the throng of people surrounding them. "But I really think it's something we should discuss in private."

The pretty intellectual shook out of her trance, and her gray eyes sparkled at the mere mention that Jason had discovered the clue.

"Fine," she said. "I'll give you a chance to explain yourself. But if you're lying, or if you try anything with me, just know that I'm armed, and I have a lot of friends in this city."

"Noted," Jason said with a nod. "You happen to know anywhere we could—"

"Come on," she said, grabbing his hand and pulling him across the plaza.

NINETEEN

JASON AND CHARLOTTE cut between two structures and climbed a set of stairs. Charlotte swiped a card key at a side entrance into the National Archeological Museum of Venice. The place was closed and dark, and Charlotte waved to the security guard as they entered.

"He's with me," she said, motioning toward Jason.

The guard gave a quick nod, then went back to leaning against a pillar.

She led him around the corner, and they entered a second-story room lined with exquisite white statues and model ships. A curtained window looked out over the lively plaza.

"You can just walk in here whenever you feel like it?" Jason said, still astonished that they'd gotten past the security guard.

"I told you, I have a lot of friends in Venice. It's like a second home to me." She scanned the archeological treasures. "Plus, I have contributed a few pieces to their collection over the years. Now, you were saying something about explaining yourself? And a clue?"

Jason gave her a brief rundown of what happened and why he'd purchased the artifact.

"So, you only bid on the item because this Nikolai Reznikov guy wanted it?"

"Exactly. We were banking on him tripping himself up and letting us in on what he was up to, and it worked. That was until we were attacked."

Charlotte shook her head in confusion. "What? You got away with the artifact, right?"

"Yeah, about that. I hate to break it to you, but it's gone."

"What do you mean, gone?"

"I mean, it's shattered to pieces."

Charlotte covered her mouth, then she narrowed her eyes, shooting daggers at Jason. "You mean to tell me you've had that jug for all of"—she glanced at her watch—"two hours, and you already broke it?"

"In my defense, it's kind of hard to hold on to anything while being tackled by a guy who could hold his own in the NFL."

"You told me you had a clue. You said it in the plaza. You said you'd found something and you needed my help figuring it out. You'd better tell me right now if you were lying." She stabbed a finger to his chest. "I'm not playing games here."

"Easy," Jason said, brushing her hand away. "I didn't lie, and I'm sure as hell not playing games. I did find a clue—or at least I think I did. I need your help figuring that out."

She held out her hands expectantly. "All right. Let's see it."

Jason slid the paper from his pocket and held it out under the light from the window. "These numbers were etched on the inside of the jug."

Charlotte snatched the paper and took a moment to inspect the digits. "It's got to be a date."

"That's what we thought, but we couldn't figure out its importance. We searched online, but nothing significant happened on that date—at least nothing was recorded or involved Captain Kidd."

Charlotte stared at the numbers, then paced back and forth across the room, tapping a finger to her lips. "But there must've been something important that happened on that date—at least for him. Something significant enough to warrant him putting it on the inside of a clay jug, which was no easy task given the technology then."

"You've studied a lot about Kidd, right?" Jason said. "I mean, you know of the legend, and you said yourself that few others do."

"I wrote my master's thesis on the Golden Age of Piracy, emphasizing the main pirates of the era and their effects on the advancement of naval warfare. I've been fascinated by their stories ever since my father gave me a copy of *A General History of the Pyrates* when I was a girl."

"So, where was Kidd in sixteen sixty-four?"

"Hispaniola." Charlotte crinkled her brow. "He would've been near modern-day Dominican Republic, Puerto Rico, then back across the Atlantic later in the year. In June, he was most likely near what is now the Virgin Islands. At least I believe so based on my recollections of his voyages."

"The Virgin Islands," Jason said as he gazed off into space.

"What is it?"

"That's where we ran into Reznikov's boys. They were blasting away a reef in the BVI off the island of Anegada."

"Searching for Kidd's treasure like that?" Charlotte said. "That's worse than trying to find a needle in a haystack."

"Yeah, well, that didn't stop them from trying . . . and severely damaging a fragile ecosystem in the process." Jason paced the room just as Charlotte had. "So, Kidd visits the islands. Then, at some point later on, he decides to secretly commemorate his favorite rum jug to his visit. Then, while on trial to be hanged years later, he alludes to a secret treasure in hopes of bargaining for his life." He shook his head, unable to come up with anything. "You sure nothing rings a bell about that date? Anything at all?"

She bit her lip. "Nothing comes to mind. But I can check over research."

"There's probably more to it. I was only able to see a piece of the jug—and briefly at that. There are probably further instructions that Reznikov and his guys are using to find it right now—like the date, followed by a little journal entry that said: 'Hey, future treasure hunters. I stashed the booty here. Spend it wisely.'" Jason turned away and began talking under his breath. "Maybe we should just head back to Anegada. The treasure's got to be somewhere in the BVI for the deranged Russian to go through all of that trouble. Or, maybe we—"

"Wait a second!" Charlotte said, snapping Jason from his tangent. "You're a genius, Mr. Wake."

He eyed her skeptically. "You can just call me Jason. And not that I don't appreciate the compliment, but how—"

"A journal entry," she said. "That has to be it."

Jason sighed. "I told you, I lost the jug."

"Yes, but I bet you managed to see the most important part of it." She looked out the window at the glowing silver moon looming overhead. "I can't believe I didn't think of it sooner. It makes complete sense. Captain William Kidd was an avid wordsmith. The guy wrote religiously, jotting down in journals and even creating his own navigation charts."

The light bulb switched on in Jason's head. "June fourteenth, sixteen sixty-four. The journal entry that Kidd's pointing us to from the grave."

"Exactly."

"Just please don't tell me they burned all of his journals after his death. Or that they've been lost to the tides of time, because that would make this whole realization very anticlimactic."

Charlotte smiled. "His journals are still intact. I read one of them years ago."

Relieved, Jason smiled. "Where are they?" Just as the question left his lips, his phone buzzed. It was Finn.

"We just spoke with Scott," Finn said, "and he says there's new activity near Anegada. He wants us to video call with him ASAP."

"We'll be right there."

"We?"

"Yeah, myself and Miss Murchison." He locked eyes with the archeologist. "And she may have just figured out our next course of action."

TWENTY

JASON AND CHARLOTTE strode into the third-story suite at the Hotel Danieli and found Alejandra and Finn hunched over the living room table. After making introductions, they placed a video call to Scott.

They'd already filled in their fearless leader on what happened at the auction and how they'd made a daring escape in the canals thanks to Finn's James Bond maneuver, so Scott went straight to his news.

"We had more blasts off Anegada today," he said. "At least three were reported."

"I figured it would've stopped after what we did to those guys in Saba," Alejandra said.

"It's safe to say it wasn't their only safe house," Scott said. "And they've clearly got more men in the area."

Jason leaned forward. "How are the islanders, Scott?"

"I just got back from The Settlement. The people are even more uneasy, and a few have already started leaving the island. As more do, I fear that the offers to buy up the land from foreign investors will become too appetizing to turn down."

"You find any links between the investors and Reznikov yet?" Jason asked.

"Murph said the connection is clear, but he's still working to find things that are concrete. Regardless, I need my team back together on the *Valiant* ASAP to prevent more blasting away of the reef. Local authorities are still acting like their hands are tied. I had a meeting scheduled with David Calvert, the governor of the British Virgin Islands, on Tortola this morning, but he canceled last minute. The whole thing reeks of corruption, and I think it's time we amped up our response."

"All right," Jason said, thinking it over. He glanced across the table at Alejandra and Finn. "You two head back to the Caribbean."

Finn shook his head. "You mean the three of us, right?"

"No," Jason said. "I'm going to Scotland to check up on a lead."

"What's in Scotland?" Alejandra asked.

"It's where William Kidd was born." Charlotte folded her arms and adjusted her glasses.

Jason nodded. "She thinks the clue is a date in Kidd's journal, but we need to move fast. With all of Reznikov's resources, I'm sure it won't take them long to figure it out as well."

Scott rubbed his chin. "So, Reznikov finds the gold, buys up the island, and turns the idyllic paradise into another stop on the cruise-ship train. That's quite the plan."

"And displaces over two hundred locals in the process," Finn added.

Jason placed his hands on the table. "But if we find it first, we can help ensure that it ends up benefiting the right people."

Scott cleared his throat and addressed the group. "All right, Jase. You check out the lead. See if you can't beat Reznikov to the punch. Miss Murchison, I'll need you to send me your info so we can run a background check like we do for everyone we work with. Jase will show you what we need and where to send it."

Charlotte gave a quick nod, and once everything was settled, they ended the call.

"You sure you two are fine going alone?" Alejandra said.

"We're just gonna drop into this museum, read a few old lines, then get out of there," Jason said. "Should be quick and easy. Besides, Scott needs you guys back on the *Valiant*. The hope is that there's still an island to save by the time we get to the bottom of this."

Finn and Alejandra strode into their prospective rooms to pack, leaving Jason and Charlotte alone in the living room.

"I guess there's no point in my asking who you guys are," Charlotte said. "Seems like you prefer the secretive approach."

Jason slid out his phone to check last-minute tickets for flights. "Look, I appreciate what you've done so far. You've been a big help, and I'm sure I'll need your assistance going forward, but if you agree to come with me, you need to accept that there are aspects about me and our group that we won't share with you."

"Like who you guys are?"

"Yes. Like that."

"Just tell me . . . what will you guys do with the treasure if you find it?"

"Like I said to the others, we'll make sure it's dispersed into the hands of those who need it."

"All of it?"

"Charlotte, I just spent two million euros on an old clay jug without knowing its significance. Not to sound arrogant, and with all due respect, but do I seem like someone who's just trying to make a quick buck?"

"No, but looks can be deceiving."

"Yeah, well, I inherited my money from a man I detested who earned the bulk of it through swindling and corrupt dealings. It doesn't mean anything to me."

Charlotte fell silent for a moment, then said, "All right, I'm satisfied. I won't ask questions or expect answers."

Jason booked their tickets, then motioned for the door. "Come on. If we're gonna visit Scotland, we're gonna need raincoats."

TWENTY-ONE

THE AIRLINER'S WHEELS touched down on the tarmac of Glasgow International Airport the following day. Having caught the earliest flights they could book, they arrived before ten in the morning and rented a black BMW to get out of the city.

They drove forty-five minutes through seas of rolling green and tree-coated hills, passing a dozen crisp golf courses along the way. The sky was thick with dark clouds, and a ten-mile-per-hour wind howled over the Celtic land. They cruised into the small, quiet town of Irvine in the historic county of Ayrshire. With a population of thirty thousand, the burgh is nestled right along the Firth of Clyde, the deepest coastal waters in the British Isles.

They passed a sign that said "Museum of Scottish Maritime History" as Jason pulled into the sprawling compound and parked in the visitor lot beside a row of massive red-brick buildings.

"It's one of the largest collections of maritime memorabilia in the world, let alone Scotland," Charlotte explained as they hopped out of the car.

They trekked past the buildings, heading toward a towering white structure that looked more like a governor's mansion than a museum. Having called ahead to let the curator know they were stopping by, Charlotte led Jason to the back entrance of the house instead of the main visitor entrance.

"I guess you have a lot of friends in Scotland, too?" Jason said, impressed as she strolled in like she owned the place.

"Miss Murchison," a round-bellied man with a Scottish accent said as they entered. He stepped away from a woman and her young daughter and moved toward Charlotte. "It's a pleasure to have an intellectual as reputable as yourself back in our humble establishment. And who's this?"

"Avery, this is Jason Wake," Charlotte said.

Jason offered his hand. "You're modest," he said, gazing around the room. "This place is incredible."

They'd barely entered the space, but Jason could already see seemingly endless rows of maritime memorabilia, including full-size ships and rows of colossal engines and propellers.

"Why, thank you. It's been the life's work of many of us here, and it was no easy feat securing the museum in Irvine in the first place. We have hundreds of exhibits currently on display, including the MV Spartan, which is the last Scottish-built steam-powered puffer. And of course, there's our Cathedral of Engineering, the former Linthouse Shipyard building that's so big it takes hours to cover the whole thing."

The man's enthusiasm was contagious, and Charlotte had to intervene to keep him from going on about the museum. "We're actually more interested in what's underground," she said.

The curator smiled. "Ah, yes. The journals of the Scottish-born Captain William Kidd. One of the most famous Scots to ever set sail. And . . . one of the most proficient." He motioned over his shoulder. "Please, if you'll just follow me this way."

He strode toward the woman and girl admiring a replica of an old steamboat. "I'll be right back," Avery said, giving the girl a kiss on her forehead. "And we'll continue the private tour."

"And then I get to captain my own foam boat?" the girl asked, referring to the museum's model boat pond.

"Of course," Avery said, patting her on the back. He spoke over his shoulder. "My granddaughter stops by every chance she gets."

They followed Avery across the back section of the structure, through a rear exit, and then across a walkway that ran parallel to a colossal brick warehouse. Once past the building, Avery pointed toward a small stone outbuilding at the back of the compound.

"Underground?" Jason whispered in Charlotte's ear.

"Yes," Avery said, somehow able to hear the question. He led them through a door, then flicked on a switch, illuminating a cramped space packed nearly floor to ceiling with random artifacts.

"Every museum has its back rooms," Avery said as he led them across the room. "Mountains of artifacts and history, just collecting dust."

Jason glanced to his left and spotted what looked like a vehicle hidden beneath a tarp. "What's that?"

The curator stopped on his heels, then pulled up a corner of the tarp, revealing a classic green automobile.

"She's a Galloway," Avery said. "One of only four thousand produced, and it was manufactured right here in Scotland. And she's a custom job. Notice the rear seats." He tapped the padded leather. "Not standard for the convertibles."

"Ever take it for a spin?" Jason said.

The Scotsman laughed. "Been many years since I opened that toolbox over there and worked on her, but she was one of the fastest cars around here in her heyday. She should still run, provided there's space to get her out." He pointed toward the items resting between the vehicle's classic bumper and the garage door. "Yep, she's a beauty," Avery added. "With a straight four, side—"

"I hate to put a damper on your parade, boys," Charlotte said. "But Kidd's . . ."

"Journals," Avery said with a smile.

He lowered the cover over the vehicle and led them to the back of the room. He surprised Jason when he opened the door and flicked on another light switch, revealing a staircase that bore into the earth and wrapped around out of sight.

"As I was saying . . . Most of the museum's items are hidden in the back. And much of the historical maritime records of Scotland are here, hidden away in the catacombs."

"Catacombs?" Jason said, amazed at what he was seeing.

Avery nodded. "It's an underground series of tunnels and rooms that were originally used to store nonperishables and act as shelters during the Second World War. And the quality of construction and surprisingly good ventilation make them a good place to store historical items."

"Like old pirate journals?" Jason inquired.

The curator smiled. "Watch your step. These stones were put into place seventy years ago."

When they reached the bottom of the stairs, Avery flicked another switch, and a row of lights illuminated a short passageway lined with doorways.

"Impressive," Jason said.

Avery led them down the corridor, then cut right into a room with tightly packed bookcases.

"This is part of the library," he said. "Some of these documents date back over a thousand years. And I have Kidd's journals over here." He shined a light on a bookcase with twenty raggedy, leather-bound books tucked into the right side.

"Which one's Kidd's?" Jason said.

"All of them. He was a meticulous writer. And thankfully, nobody saw fit to destroy the disgraced pirate's works after he died." Avery pulled out one of the journals. "You said sixteen sixty-four, correct?" When Charlotte nodded, he opened it, carefully leafed through the pages, then set it on a metal table and switched on a lamp. "Here you are. This is the journal he used from sixty-two until sixty-eight. He didn't write as much in those early years of his adult life, what with his being a low-ranking seaman during those periods. Not a lot of time or energy to scribble down your thoughts after rigging lines and swathing decks all day. It's amazing he was able to even keep a journal and maintain it in such good shape given the quality of life for young sailors back then. These were all taken from Kidd's house in New York after he was hanged."

A voice echoed down the corridor, calling Avery's name. Jason recognized it as the man's young grand-daughter, who'd apparently gotten curious about where her grandfather had ventured off to.

"Please, excuse me," Avery said. "There's a ram-bunctious little one I promised could command a mod-el-boat fleet. Feel free to take your time, and you know where to find answers if you have any questions."

"Thank you, Avery," Charlotte said. "I owe you one."

"After all that you and your father have done for this museum over the years, if anything, it is I who owe *you* one." He strolled out from the dark library, disappearing into the main passageway.

"I didn't realize you were such a force in the aca-demic community," Jason said. "Though, I'm not sur-prised, given what little I've observed of you so far."

He noticed her blush a little before composing herself and turning her undivided attention on the journal.

"Okay," she said, tracing a finger over the faded pages coated in lines of black-inked cursive. "Here's sixteen sixty-four."

Jason observed her as she handled the artifact with the precision of a surgeon. He had a hard time believing that the words on the page were handwritten three hundred and fifty years earlier. The fact that the pages were in such great shape and that the journals hadn't been destroyed by one way or another, was nothing short of astonishing.

Jason and Charlotte let out a collective sigh of relief as they landed upon June 14th.

"Looks like my theory might be right," Charlotte said.

But after laying eyes on the journal entry, it was polished crystal clear that they weren't home free yet. Kidd's small writing took up nearly half the page— all things that the famous pirate had jotted down on that day alone.

"He sure was thorough," Jason said.

"It was good practice. Smart sailors of the day would write down what they saw and experienced. That way, whenever they returned to the same place, they could refresh themselves on the geography and avoid potentially dangerous waters or islands." Using a magnifying lens, Charlotte leaned over the journal and began reading it aloud.

TWENTY-TWO

"UPON MY LIFE,"** Charlotte said, reading from Kidd's diary, "providence has once again spared me from an abominable fate. Following a hostile encounter with natives, the captain set course for a small island in The Virgins where fresh water was rumored. But a storm overtook us and cast our ship upon the reef. With the winds and waves and rain beating down, myself and four other survivors climbed into a skiff with hopes of reaching the distant black shore of the flat island.

"We were nearing our destination when the mighty swells became too much for our craft to bear. A powerful tempest slammed our hull into a shallow reef, causing the timbers to crack and splinter to pieces, and tossing us into the sea. Thrashing in the chaos of the seething ocean, I struggled to aid my comrades and hold tight to whatever we could. My good friend Camdyn Blair, whom I'd first set sail with from Dundee, was killed before my eyes and swallowed up by the raging torrent. Certain that the end was near, but pleading for Mother Nature and the fates to be merciful, we held on, sure that every wave would cast our helpless bodies against the reef and finish us off.

"It was while we were kicking desperately for the shore that a powerful undertow unlike anything I've ever experienced sucked the three of us still alive beneath the waves. We fought with everything we had to escape the raging current, but our attempts were futile. The ocean wanted us, and I knew in that dark and turbulent moment that our time had come.

"We jostled this way and that, slamming against rocks and spinning uncontrollably, having no choice but to give in to the ocean's harsh demands. With my lungs burning and the clock ticking down on my life, I felt the end grabbing hold of me. Then, by some miraculous twist of fate, my body was thrown against a sloping rock, where I tumbled out from the sea and onto dry land.

"The raging chaos subsided, and I heard only my pounding heart and gasping breaths. Swallowed in a void of inky blackness, I knew not where I was or if I was even alive. Then, the sounds of splashing water filled the air. I crawled toward the sound and helped one of my comrades up onto the rock. Like myself, he coughed out seawater, then gasped as he looked around. It was only by the sound of his voice that I recognized him as Sherman Edwards, a midshipman three years my senior.

"We knew not where we were. It was too dark and quiet for us to have reached a beach. In the distance overhead, we heard the muffled rumbles of the angry sea that by some miracle we'd escaped. With no light to guide us, we had no choice but to stumble our way through the darkness, our bodies battered, and our minds struggling to comprehend that we were still breathing. The going was slow and tedious. We climbed over slippery rock faces, winding our way blindly and hoping that Mother Nature wasn't toying with our lives.

"It felt like an eternity in that cave. And we were certain that we'd reach a dead end at every turn. That we'd realize we were stuck there, and unlike the rest of the unfortunate crew, we'd perish slowly of thirst. But the cave soon opened, and we stumbled into a wide-open space where the air was cool and echoed when we spoke. On the other side of the cavern, we splashed into a pool of water that rose to our waists. Then, the way came to an abrupt halt.

"Feeling around the smooth rock face, I found a pocket where the water dropped deeper. To our amazement, we realized that it wasn't seawater. It was fresh. And though it was brackish, we took the discovery as a good sign. With our options exhausted, I held my breath and ventured into the depths. It took three tries, but I eventually felt my way into a cave that cut under the rock face then rose skyward. Kicking with everything I had, I broke free and sucked in the best-tasting air of my life.

"Looking around, I realized that I'd surfaced in a lake fringed by palm trees. The storm was still raging, but I cheered in pure jubilation, having somehow survived the ordeal. After returning to Edwards and leading him out, we took shelter on the island and were picked up by a search party three days later.

"While looking for survivors, Edwards and I found the powerful current and the opening in the reef we'd been sucked into during the storm. We mapped it out as five hundred meters from the eastern shore near the southeastern tip of the island. Just before the reef cuts and extends out into open water, there is a crack at the base of a wall of limestone that rises and nearly pierces the surface at low tide. This marks the barely noticeable entrance into the cave that saved our lives that day.

"Later that evening, we burned the bodies of our lost crewmembers on the beach while drinking to their memories. And Edwards and I drank to the cave which had liberated us from the jaws of the raging beast."

TWENTY-THREE

JASON AND CHARLOTTE fell silent after she finished off the journal entry, both captivated by Kidd's daring tale and the description of a secret cave's location.

Finally, Charlotte spoke. "I'm gonna take a stab in the dark and say this island Kidd is referring to is the same island where you were investigating the blast incidents."

Jason smiled. "Anegada. The description certainly matches up. A low-lying island surrounded by reefs." He paused a moment, taking in the story, then wrapped an arm around Charlotte. "I think Captain Kidd just told us from the grave where he hid his famous treasure. After three hundred and fifty years, it's time for his little trail to be followed. It's time we find this cave."

Slipping out his phone, Jason took pictures of the text, paying special attention to the lines describing the opening into the cave. The description wasn't complicated, and Jason was confident he could find the place without the pictures, but he snapped them just to be sure.

Once finished, he dropped the phone back into his pocket, and Charlotte shut the journal and clicked off the lamp. As they moved back to the bookshelf, they heard voices echoing from down the passageway. With Charlotte still clutching the journal, they gravitated toward the entryway and listened as the voices grew louder.

"I don't have time for games, old man," a harsh voice snarled.

Jason recognized it instantly. He could still see the wretch's face—still feel his breath when he told him back in Venice that it was over.

"Where are they?" Boris grunted. "And where's Kidd's journal?"

"They're not here," Avery replied. "I don't know who—"

"You're a terrible liar." Boris coughed, and the sounds of heavy footsteps reverberated down into the catacombs. "Wake! I know you're down there! Get out here now with Kidd's journal, or I'll blow this man's brains out."

Jason's eyes sprang wide, then he focused on Charlotte. When she strode toward the doorway, resolved to save her friend from the grips of the deadly Russian criminal, Jason stopped her.

"No," he whispered, "I'll handle this. You hide."

When she was about to protest, Jason snatched the journal from her hands. Instead of taking it to the Russian, he unzipped her backpack and secured the old book inside it. Grabbing a different old leather-bound book from the shelf, he pointed toward the back of the room. "Stay here and keep hidden. I'll handle this."

"By yourself? There's—"

"The important thing is protecting you and Avery and making sure Reznikov doesn't get his hands on the treasure."

"You're forcing my hand, Wake!" Boris shouted.

Jason spun on his heels with the book in his grip and dashed for the corridor. "Wait!" he shouted back. He exited the library and peeked down the walkway just as a gunshot shook the air, echoing down into the tunnels. Jason's mouth dropped open, and his eyes froze in anger and terror as Avery's body collapsed into view, tumbling down the stairs and coming to rest against the stone floor. Jason gasped as blood pooled out from a bullet wound to the museum curator's forehead.

An intense rage boiled over inside him as he stared at the dead man on the ground. A brutal murder of an innocent man, and right before his eyes. He blinked as footsteps again echoed from up the stairway. When Boris appeared, Jason instinctively reached for the Glock in his waistband.

"Not so fast, Wake," Boris said, smiling sinisterly.

Right on Boris's heels, two more men appeared, holding tight to the woman and the young girl. The mother was frantic, her eyes welling with tears as she saw Avery's body.

"You open fire, and we'll kill these two, as well," Boris growled. "Now . . . drop your weapon."

Jason gritted his teeth, unable to take his eyes off the woman and young girl. He did as Boris asked, relaxing his grip on the pistol and letting it fall to his feet.

Boris's smile broadened. "Now, the journal," he said, holding out an open hand. "Give it here."

Seeing no other choice but to give in to the guy's demands, Jason walked across the passageway. With every step, a voice in his head told him Boris couldn't be trusted. It told him that even if he gave the Russian what he wanted, he'd kill the woman and child out of spite. He needed to act. He needed to do something.

Boris stomped down and met Jason at the base of the stairs. Under the light of the passageway, Jason caught his first glimpse of the man's rough face and the grotesque wound to his left cheek from the clay shard.

"Like I told you in Italy, Wake, you will lose in the end. You will lose, and all of your attempts will be futile. My boss and I always come out on top."

He held out his left hand expectantly, and Jason handed him the book. Keeping his eyes locked on Jason, Boris handed the book to one of the henchmen at his back.

"Let them go, Boris," Jason said. "You have what you came for. No need to drag them into this."

Boris thought for a moment. "I am a man of my word." He motioned toward the guy, and he let go of the woman and girl. Gasping with fear, they both took off up the stairs, disappearing from view.

"Yes, I am a man of my word," the Russian said, staring back at Jason. "And like I said, Wake, you are finished."

Boris raised his pistol, aiming it right at Jason's forehead. With his finger on the trigger, he flexed slightly and eyed Jason with an intense gaze. Jason matched it, unblinking and unafraid.

"I must say, I'm impressed by your courage. Most men falter and cower and beg for mercy when I confront them."

"You'd better stop stalling and pull that damn trigger, Boris," Jason spat. "'Cause you and I both know that it's the only way you could take me down."

The Russian snickered. "Your arrogance deceives you, punk. Nikolai told me about you. How you were raised with a damn silver spoon. You think you can take me because you spent a year at your country's soft little secret training facility? I was born in turmoil, Wake. Cold and dark and hard. I was pounded time and time again, beaten to a pulp even before my youth. But this beating was like the hammer striking the sword—a furnace that forged me into a weapon—a force more powerful than anything you've ever come up against."

"Yet you cower behind your gun," Jason retorted, holding his intense stare on the Russian.

Boris lowered his pistol. "Or maybe you aren't courageous at all. Maybe . . . you want death. Maybe something happened in your past that haunts you, and you can't escape it."

Jason narrowed his gaze, his heart pounding in his chest.

"Maybe you want to see your precious Emilia again," Boris continued, his words slow and sharp, like cold steel penetrating Jason's flesh. He savored the young man's reaction. "You're precious Emilia who was taken from you by—"

Unable to take it any longer, Jason lunged forward and reached for the weapon in Boris's right hand. The muscular Russian expected the sudden burst of recklessness. He whirled laterally and slammed a fist into the side of Jason's body, causing the American to falter backward and stumble against the wall. When the two men at Boris's back raised their weapons in unison, their leader called them off.

"He's mine," Boris spat, then tossed his handgun aside. "You've chosen the slow and painful way. You'll be wishing I put a bullet in your skull by the time I'm done with you."

The colossal man kept his eyes locked on Jason as he stomped down the final step. When he hit the bottom, he arched his back and bent his knees into a fighting stance. Jason did the same, gearing up for the bout.

Enraged by the sight of the dead museum curator still bleeding out on the floor beside them, Jason made the first move. He threw a rapid flurry of punches, Boris avoiding or blocking them all before grabbing Jason by the throat. He was stronger, bigger, and more experienced than Jason.

"You'll have to do better than that, Wake," he snarled.

When Jason lifted his hands to break free of the hold, Boris let go then jarred the American with a punch to the gut. Jason rolled with the blow, then swung his right leg, but the quick Russian hopped over the swipe, dropped back, and threw a kick of his own, pounding his heel into Jason's chest. The younger man flew backward, smashing into a locked door and breaking the wood from its hinges.

Jason crashed into a dark room, landing on the shattered door. Going with his momentum, the American rolled backward twice before jumping to his feet. The moment he gathered himself, Boris filled the doorway, striding casually into the room filled with shelves of artifacts.

Jason engaged his foe with reckless abandon, throwing two more punches before striking the Russian with a knee to his hip. Boris grunted from the violent blow. Furious, he lifted Jason off the ground and tossed him into a nearby shelf. The metal frame of the rack creaked and gave way, and objects fell free as it toppled to the floor. Rolling right and shuffling behind a second massive shelf, Jason fought through the pain and disappeared from the angry Russian's view.

"It's useless to fight me, punk," Boris spat. "I've fought men much harder than you time and time again. No training can match experience. And few men have killed as much as I have."

When Boris stomped around the corner, his eyes bulged as Jason flew into view. Running full speed, Jason jumped and grabbed the corner of one of the still-standing shelves' metal frames. Redirecting his momentum, he swung his body toward the Russian. The brute tried to dodge the blow, but Jason was too fast and caught him off guard. Jason drove his heels into flesh, knocking Boris off his feet and sending him flying into the concrete wall at his back. His hulking frame struck hard, and he grunted as he fell to a knee.

As Jason landed, the Russian quickly collected himself. When he stormed toward the American again, he snatched a twelve-inch knife from his hip. "You're not making this any easier on yourself, Wake," he growled, pointing the tip of his blade forward. "For that one, I'm gonna kill your little lady friend, too. I know she's down here, and she can't hide from us."

Jason scouted for a weapon of his own, but before he could find one, Boris bolted toward him, swinging his razor-sharp steel back and forth. With no other option, Jason went on the defensive, ducking and bouncing back to avoid being sliced to shreds. Boris yelled, faked Jason out, then caught the American's left thigh with a swipe, cutting a shallow gash across the flesh.

Jason yelled out and nearly collapsed from the blow. Thinking his adversary was finished, Boris laughed and drove forward, stabbing the blade toward Jason's gut. With pain screaming from his leg, Jason rolled left, snatched a book from the shelf beside him, then held it up.

Boris stabbed the knife through the hardcover, the tip nearly breaking all the way through. Before Boris could yank his weapon free, Jason twisted the book forcefully, tearing the weapon from his hands, then tossed the book aside. Boris lunged at Jason, grabbed a fistful of his shirt, and then slammed him against the shelf. He punched Jason twice more, nearly knocking him unconscious before hurling him toward the entryway.

Jason smacked against the floor and rolled onto his side. He struggled to breathe and move, his mind hazy, and his body burning in pain.

Boris sauntered over to his knife and ripped it from the book. "You know, I expected more from a man who dedicated his life to avenging the murder of his little girlfriend." Boris stomped across the room, knelt, and grabbed Jason by his collar. Holding the blade with his right hand, Boris pinned Jason into the ground and held him in place. "I guess maybe you didn't love her very much."

Jason snarled and tried to fight back with everything he had, but Boris kept him pressed to the cold floor with the shiny blade right over Jason's body. "Any last words, Wake?"

The moment the question left his lips, a gunshot shook the space to life.

When Boris looked up, he heard one of his men yell out in pain.

"Take cover!" his other henchman yelled, firing off retaliatory rounds.

With Boris's attention drawn to the commotion in the walkway, Jason gripped a sharp, splintered piece of the broken door resting beside him. Just as Boris fixed his sights back down and flexed, ready to finish Jason off with his blade, the American impaled the wood clean through the Russian's neck.

Boris's eyes grew massive, and he rasped desperately. Blood dripped down from both sides of his neck, splattering onto Jason's chest as the big man shook and his strength faded. Adjusting his body, Jason shoved the Russian off him. Boris fell onto his back, dropping his knife and clutching the splintered piece of wood with both hands. Hearing shuffling feet just outside the doorway, Jason grabbed the knife and bolted for the entryway. He reached it just as Charlotte appeared, then lowered the weapon with a gasp.

"Jason!" she said, wrapping her arms around him. "I took down one of them. I couldn't leave you. I had to—"

"It won't matter," Boris spat, struggling to get the words out. In his right hand, he held a cellphone, its screen illuminated. "My men are locking this place down, along with everyone in it. Then they're gonna burn you all alive!"

TWENTY-FOUR

JASON BOLTED ACROSS the room, ripped the phone from Boris's dying hand, and stared at the message that the Russian had just sent.

"Plan B" was all it said.

Before Jason could ask what it meant, Boris exhaled his last breath and went motionless. Knowing they had to get moving, Jason grabbed Boris's handgun, and the two raced through the door, down the corridor, and up the stairs. When they reached the top, they were welcomed by thick clouds of smoke wafting under the door.

Keeping Charlotte back, Jason lunged forward and threw open the door, allowing a plume to break free and gust into his face. He wafted the smoke from around him and stepped back. As it cleared, they covered their mouths and then heard screams up ahead.

Flames spread along both corners of the structure and rapidly climbed up toward the rafters. Jason and Charlotte bolted across the room, heading toward the sounds of the woman and child yelling frantically. They cut to the front and found the woman pounding against the structure's metal door. With the fire and smoke on the other side of the room, Jason and Charlotte coughed, caught their breath, and looked around.

"We're locked in!" the woman shrieked between coughs.

"We're gonna die in here!" the little girl screamed, bawling as she covered her face.

Jason scanned around as best as he could through the toxic clouds. There appeared to be just the one door in and out, and after pounding the thin metal with two vigorous kicks, it was clear that Boris's remaining thug had barricaded it from the outside.

With the flames growing in intensity and the young child panicking, Jason dropped down beside her. He placed his hands on her shoulders and stared into her tear-filled eyes. "We're going to get out of this, you hear me?" he said, his voice raised over the roaring flames. He coughed and cleared his throat. "But I need you to be strong. I need you to be brave."

The little girl wiped away tears as Jason rose and then pointed toward the base of the door. "Keep low, and stay here," he said.

When the woman and girl did as he instructed, Jason turned back to face the intensifying blaze.

"Where are you going?" Charlotte asked him.

"To find a way out of here." He hustled across the room, cutting into the back and trying the knob on the rear door. It was also locked, and a few solid slams of his shoulder convinced him he wasn't getting out that way. Storming back through the smoke, he burst out into the main room and scoured the place as his eyes burned. The structure had no windows. It was filled with piles of seemingly random artifacts, many of them wooden and just ready to combust and spread the fire. At the other side of the room, he spotted shattered kerosene lamps in the corner, the contents no doubt used to set the place ablaze.

Searching the place frantically and hoping to find a crowbar or blowtorch or some other means of getting out of there, his eyes rested on the covered classic automobile in the middle of the room. Stumbling toward the vehicle, Jason threw off the cover.

"One of the fastest cars of her time," Avery had boasted.

With nowhere else to turn, and with the fire quickly spreading, Jason climbed into the driver's seat. He reached for the ignition, but there were no keys. He searched in the center console, the glovebox, and under the floor mats, but came up empty on all counts. Feeling the heat and coughing from the smoke, Jason sprang over to the workbench and threw open the lid of the toolbox. Grabbing a flathead screwdriver and a pair of needle-nose pliers, he dashed back to the car and crawled under the steering wheel.

"Jason!" Charlotte shouted, searching for him while shielding her mouth from the smoke.

"Over here!" Jason belted out as he quickly removed the screws holding the steering column cover in place.

She followed his voice, practically stumbling into the side of the car before seeing his body contorted under the dashboard. "What are you doing?"

With the screws removed, Jason fumbled the cover open, then reached for a cluster of wires. Sifting through the lines, he pinched the red wire, which he hoped was to the battery, then pulled it free and used the pliers to strip the coating off its end. Coughing away the smoke, he felt through the rest of the wires, trying to find the one that led to the starter. With no time to check the manual, Jason picked a blue one and stripped away the rubber coating.

"Go and get the mother and daughter!" Jason shouted.

Charlotte struggled to stay conscious as she leaned against the side of the Galloway. "Do you have any idea what you're doing?"

Jason shimmied out and stared her in the eyes through the smoke. "Just go and get them. Climb in the back. It's our only chance."

She did as he said, slowly navigating her way back across the room.

Contorting his body back under the wheel, Jason stripped the second wire and held his breath as he touched the copper strands together. "Come on, baby."

There was a long list of things that could go wrong, but he shoved the negative thoughts out of his mind. He didn't have time for them or what they had to offer. He had no choice but to make it work.

A spark shot up when the two coils collided, and Jason heard the engine groan but fail to turn over. "Come on, come on!" he said, choking as he sparked the wires together a second time.

The moment the engine turned over, Jason let go of the wires and shoved a hand onto the gas pedal, revving the motor to keep it from stalling out. The engine roared before grumbling and gurgling and sputtering to life. Slowly, the vintage machine revitalized itself, pounding and popping to a low and steady hum.

He let off the gas and crawled out from under the dash just as Charlotte and the two others arrived.

"Jason!" Charlotte said, coughing violently as she reached the idling car.

Jason helped the mom and daughter into the back, then practically carried Charlotte into the passenger seat. They were all rapidly approaching the edge of consciousness, and the flames had grown and were now raging in a hot inferno right at their backs.

Jason scrambled into the driver's seat and grabbed the shifter with one hand and the wheel with the other. Feeling the heat at his back, and barely able to see anything through the thick plumes of smoke, he put the classic car in gear and struck the gas pedal. The old engine groaned, and the tires spun, struggling for a moment to gain traction before jolting them forward. To their right, a massive model ship was in flames, and the mast splintered and fell just as they motored by it.

"Come on . . . come on!" Jason shouted.

The burning wreckage fell toward them like a falling tree, and to a chorus of screams and cries, the flaming heavy log slammed home, striking the Galloway's tailgate and jarring the frame as the mast rumbled to the floor. Jason mashed the gas pedal, driving them right through a shelf of artifacts and making a beeline for the front door.

"Hold on!" he shouted as the door appeared through the smoke.

The Galloway struck the door, shearing it from its frame and taking the whole doorway with it. When they burst free from the old structure, Jason slammed into the dashboard, nearly flying from his seat on impact. Gripping tight to the wheel and keeping his foot on the gas, they finally escaped into the clear Scottish air.

With the smoke billowing out and the structure erupting in flames at their back, Jason spotted Boris's thug standing where the grass met the parking lot. Clutching the old book, the thug jumped back at the sight of the classic car bursting out of the burning building.

Jason cut the wheel sharply and floored the gas pedal again. They drifted across the field, and the man was barely able to attempt a dive out of the way before Jason drove right into him, pummeling the criminal's body with the grill. Sprawled out over the hood, he slipped down the frame and was trampled by the wheels.

Letting off the gas, Jason braked to a stop at the edge of the parking lot, spinning the vehicle around so that they faced the man's motionless body and the fiery structure beyond him.

TWENTY-FIVE

STILL COUGHING AND wiping his stinging eyes, Jason turned back for the first time since breaking free of the inferno. The woman and daughter were curled up in the back seat, shaking in fear and fighting to clear their lungs, but alive. Charlotte was motionless, her head resting on the seat and facing him. She was pale, her face was coated in sweat, and her hair was a mess.

Jason checked her pulse, relieved to feel the vein throbbing at the side of her neck. Climbing out of the car, he ran around the vehicle, opened the passenger door, and unbuckled Charlotte's seatbelt, then eased her onto the grass and tried his best to snap her out of it.

"She saved us," the woman said with her young daughter in her arms. "We were swallowed up, and she grabbed us and led us to the car."

Jason patted Charlotte's cheek and repeated her name. He held his ear over her mouth, and realizing that she wasn't breathing, began CPR right away. He gave her thirty chest compressions before exhaling two breaths into her mouth and starting over.

A storm of sirens blared in the distance, growing louder every second. Panic started to set in as Jason began the third round of CPR. Charlotte still wasn't breathing, and her pulse was getting weaker with every passing second. He pleaded for her to wake up, his fatigue and pain and emotions taking hold.

The woman and daughter climbed out and sat in the grass beside him, tears welling up as they held each other, hoping for Charlotte to wake up.

Starting more chest compressions, Jason continued repeating her name, trying to will her back. Charlotte choked suddenly, her eyes springing wide and her head tilting forward. Jason sighed as he stopped CPR, nearly breaking down from happiness as she caught her breath. He helped prop her up as she heaved the dangerous amounts of smoke from her lungs, clearing it out with the coastal air.

After struggling for air, she gazed around in shock.

"You're all right," Jason said with his arm wrapped around her.

She fixated on him, then pressed her face into his chest. "I blacked out," she gasped. "I don't remember anything after collapsing into the car."

Jason pulled her in tighter, and the woman and girl sat down beside them as the flames spread, spewing out from the building and swallowing it whole. The sounds of raging fire and groaning metal filled the air. Thick streams of smoke billowed up into the clouded sky, carried off by the steady breeze.

It wasn't long before fire trucks and ambulances whined onto the scene. The huge red rigs backed up close to the blaze, and the firefighters went to work dousing the inferno with thick streams of water from different angles. The four of them watched as the fire ensued and the roof collapsed into itself.

Firefighters and paramedics ushered them farther away and checked each of them over. Before they could be questioned by police, Jason led Charlotte across the lot and into their parked BMW.

They buckled in, and Jason started up the engine. "You sure you don't need to go to a hospital?"

"Me? What about you? You're the one who went toe to toe with that big Russian. Look at yourself, Wake."

She flipped down the driver-side mirror, allowing Jason to examine himself for the first time since the violent encounter with Boris. His face was bruised and scratched, his clothes tattered and covered with black burn marks. But the cut to his left thigh was the worst—a long gash that had been bleeding out steadily since Boris had slashed him with his knife. Fortunately, the paramedics applied temporary bandages that had stopped the bleeding for the time being.

"I'm fine for now," he said, putting the car in gear and driving them out of the lot.

They cruised back north to Glasgow and booked a hotel so they could clean up. While looking over his wounds, Jason examined his leg and knew that stitches were in order. With his adrenaline worn off, he winced as he staggered to the second bedroom, and hearing the shower running, rapped his knuckles against the open bathroom door.

"Charlotte, could I get your help?" he said over the splashing water.

When she didn't reply, he poked his head in and saw her sitting in the shower. She was still fully dressed with her back against the tiled wall, letting the steaming downpour cascade over her body and drench her clothes.

Still dressed as well, Jason stepped into the shower and sat down beside her. Water soaked his hair and trickled down his face. Charlotte kept her eyes forward as he wrapped his arms around her. She leaned in but kept her shell-shocked gaze forward. Her adrenaline had also faded.

"I've known Avery since I was little," she said, struggling to get the words out. "He was on an expedition with my father, and he gave me an Egyptian bracelet they'd uncovered. He was a good man and a brilliant historian. And they killed him, just like that. Without a moment's thought. And for what?"

She sniffled and lowered her head. Jason didn't say anything. There was nothing he could say. He knew as well as anyone that some things just need time, and even then, the scar never fully heals. They were facing off against evil adversaries who murdered without remorse.

He remembered what Boris had told him before their final confrontation: "Few men have killed as much as I have."

And Boris would've continued to end innocent lives for years had they not put a stop to it. Avery's death hadn't been in vain, but the fact that the happy, passionate museum curator had been an innocent casualty gave Jason a sick feeling deep in his stomach.

They sat under the warm waterfall for a half hour, and when Charlotte calmed down enough to think clearer, she stitched Jason up. They changed and booked the soonest flight they could back to the Caribbean.

TWENTY-SIX

THOUGH THE INCIDENT at the maritime museum ended in a disaster and claimed the curator's life, it also resulted in discovering the location where Captain William Kidd had buried his treasure. Charlotte still had the notebook, and there in the record of young Kidd's travels was the secret to putting an end to all that Reznikov was up to. They'd taken down his right-hand man, but if Jason had learned anything over the years, it was that you can't underestimate criminal masterminds—especially ones like Nikolai Reznikov, who couldn't care less about anyone but himself.

Jason and Charlotte checked into their first-class seats aboard a Boeing 777, and the wheels took off from the Glasgow tarmac just after seven. Jason got ahold of his team on the *Valiant*, and after receiving an update on the current state of the island and surrounding reef, informed them of what they'd found in Kidd's journal.

"Five hundred meters from the eastern shore near the southeastern tip of the island," Jason said, reading straight from Kidd's journal. "Just before the reef cuts and extends out into open water, there is a crack at the base of a wall of limestone that rises up and nearly pierces the surface at low tide. That's where the entrance to this cave supposedly is."

Finn had the chart of Anegada and its surrounding waters displayed on the touchscreen table in the *Valiant*'s command room. "That's right about here," he said, pointing where the southeastern section of Horseshoe Reef broke off and veered out into the deep blue. "On the opposite side from where Reznikov's boys have been blowing up the reef."

"You want us to wait for you, Jase?" Alejandra asked.

"No way. As much as I'd love to be there when this cave is discovered, it's important that we find and claim this treasure as soon as possible."

While Jason wrapped up the call, Charlotte slid the door open and appeared wearing navy blue sweatpants and a white T-shirt.

"I'm gonna try and get some sleep," Jason said to the team after glancing at the woman. "After the day we had, and with the long days still ahead, we're gonna need it."

"We won't haul up the entire treasure without you, Jase," Finn said.

"And we'll be sure to keep you updated when your plane lands with the progress," Scott said.

They ended the call, and Charlotte sat on the edge of his bed. "They're going into the cave, then?"

"As soon as they're able to get the sub in the water."

"You guys have a submarine?"

"A mini one, yeah. Hopefully, we can find it soon and put an end to this. But Reznikov won't go down easy, and he sure as hell won't do so without a fight. I hope we scared him off, but we may have just angered him even more."

"He needs to be stopped, Jason. One way or another. Even if he fails with this scheme, he'll just conjure up another. And more innocents like Avery will pile up behind him."

Jason focused forward, then brushed back his hair. "I know."

"You've met Reznikov before, haven't you?"

"He was friends with my father. Or, more like business associates, I guess. They worked together on a few of those schemes before he passed."

"Were you close to him? To your father, I mean."

"No. We never were."

"I'm sorry. I couldn't imagine not being on good terms with my father." She slid down on the bed and slowly drew closer to Jason. She went on about her father and all of the trips they'd taken around the world. She talked about the locations and artifacts she'd discovered, the places she'd lived, and the various museums and colleges she'd worked for. It surprised Jason to learn that she was a professor of archeology at Boston University, but she spent most of her time in the field. She was an accomplished woman, a force to be reckoned with, and Jason couldn't help himself from being attracted to her.

After an hour of talking and eating a meal of chicken, potatoes, and green beans delivered from the attendant, Charlotte fell silent a moment. Knowing there was something on her mind, Jason asked what it was.

"What Boris said back at the museum," she said. "About Emilia. I heard that from down the corridor. Who was she?"

Jason cleared his throat, then peered out the window and into the black sky. "She was my girlfriend. I was about to propose to her when she was taken from me. That was almost two years ago in Paris."

"Two years ago in Paris. You mean—"

"Yes. The terrorist bombing. She was on the train."

"Jeez, Jason, I'm so sorry. How did you find out?"

"I was there. I stood beside the tracks at the Gare du Nord train station when it happened. The blast knocked me back, tossing me to the ground. When I looked back up, all that remained was fiery wreckage."

Charlotte paused, letting the gravity of the realization sink in. "What did you do?"

"I was a zombie for three weeks. Didn't do much of anything. Didn't feel much of anything. Then, a wave of intensity swept over me, and my despair turned to anger, and then a burning resolve to get the men who killed her."

"Did you?"

Jason nodded.

Charlotte squeezed Jason tighter and lay on his chest. "So now, this is what you do?"

"Yes, this is what I do."

Jason sighed and downed a sip of water.

"Are you all right?" she asked.

"Yeah, I just haven't talked about it in a while."

They lay there, wrapped up in each other's arms. It wasn't long before the arduous day, combined with the rhythmic hum of the plane's engines, lulled Charlotte to sleep. Jason stayed up with his thoughts, running through everything that had happened the past few days.

As he admired the view of the southern tip of Greenland, its icy shores glowing beneath the half-moon and the clear night sky, his thoughts drifted to Reznikov. He remembered the Russian well from their brief visits when he was younger, and seeing and conversing with the Russian criminal back in Venice had taken him back there.

Nikolai Reznikov was a man who brought corruption and pain to others everywhere he went, and like Jason's father, he needed to be stopped. Jason vowed that treasure or no treasure, he'd take Reznikov down. If he had to track the lowlife to the ends of the Earth, he'd put an end to him and his posse for good.

TWENTY-SEVEN

FINN PILOTED THE dark silver minisub along the edges of the reef, he and Alejandra keeping their eyes peeled through the large, concave front window of the craft. At fourteen feet long and eight feet wide, the advanced submersible could reach a depth of up to a mile, cruise up to ten miles per hour through the water, and had a mission time of twelve hours. In addition to the extended bottom time compared to scuba, the sub also allowed them to carefully observe, record, and survey the underwater domain from the comfort of leather seats.

Gripping the joystick, Finn accelerated around a patch of coral, scaring away a school of tropical fish that broke around them as they rounded the corner.

"We're roughly five hundred meters from the island's southeastern shore," Alejandra said, reading the description Jason had sent them from Kidd's journal. She pointed toward a ledge of limestone off their starboard side. "And that's clearly the wall that Kidd was referring to."

"And we're nearing the spot where the reef branches out and stops running parallel to the island," Finn added, glancing at the GPS image of their position.

Observing the marine features around them carefully, they watched as a southern stingray glided past them, swimming just above the sand and heading out to deeper water.

Finn navigated them up into shallower water as they followed the limestone wall. They were just thirty feet down when he spotted what appeared to be a small crack at the base of the rock. The tiny dark line was surrounded by thick patches of coral and various marine growth.

"This has to be it, right?" Finn said.

Alejandra continued reading the words from Kidd's journal. "There is a crack at the base of a wall of limestone that rises up and nearly pierces the surface at low tide."

Both she and Finn leaned forward, gazing up toward the surface. Finn flicked on two additional exterior lights, beaming two powerful bright streaks toward the top of the limestone. Small whitecaps sloshed just above the rock.

"Sure looks like this is it," Alejandra said, scanning the area. "And it's the only feature nearby that matches the description."

Finn eased the craft down through a gentle combination of ballast tank control and use of the thrusters. Stopping just a few feet from the sandy bottom, he shifted their position to aim the forward lights into the wall of rock. They scanned every inch of the rock face, searching for any sign of an opening, but they couldn't see anything.

"There might not be an opening anymore," Finn said after five minutes of searching. "This description from Kidd is over three hundred years old. The reef we're looking at now is vastly different than the one he would've seen back then. The opening into the cave might not even exist anymore."

"Maybe we should've pulled a chapter out of Reznikov's playbook and brought explosives," Alejandra said. Seeing Finn's stunned reaction, she patted the Venezuelan on the back. "Just kidding." She pointed toward a unique coral formation to the right of the base of the crack in the rock. "What about over there?

Can you get a good view, or you want me to don some scuba gear and get closer?"

"I got it," Finn said, expertly bringing the submersible to where she pointed.

They lightly touched the sandy seafloor, Finn aimed the lights, and they both pored over nothing but solid rock face.

Finn sighed, then reviewed the chart in his lap. "Maybe here?" he said, stabbing a finger at the screen.

"We already searched there," Alejandra said, leaning over to look at the chart. She peered back through the window. "It has to be here. Let's go over it one more time."

Finn shrugged. He loved taking the little vehicle out for a spin any chance he could get. He brought them around to the front where the two rocks met, then swayed back and forth, scanning the lights. It was six in the evening, and the sun was barely hovering over the western sky, but the lights still helped thirty feet beneath the surface. When Finn reached the bottom again, he leveled the sub and analyzed the chart.

"Anything, guys?" Scott said through the sub's radio.

"We think we're here," Finn replied, "but we can't find any openings."

"Roger that. Let's get divers in the water and see if we can get a closer look."

"Copy. Heading back." He turned to Alejandra. "Guess play time's over. Time to blow some bubbles."

He hit the reverse thrusters, accelerating the submersible backward away from the ledge. As the bubbly wake churned from the craft's propellers, it picked up a handful of sediment and tossed it against the coral. A spiny-tailed lobster startled out from its hiding place turned and whipped its tail out under itself, whooshing its red body through the water. It flew out from under a rock and disappeared under a large plate of table coral near the base of the ledge.

"Wait!" Alejandra said, holding up a hand.

Finn let go of the accelerator, then peeked frantically through the glass as the craft slowed to a stop. "What is it? You see more of Reznikov's thugs?"

"No, not that," Alejandra said, focusing intently through the window. She pointed toward the base of the ledge. "There!"

Finn raised his eyebrows at her. "What about it?"

"You didn't see it? That bug disappeared under that red growth of coral right there."

Catching onto Alejandra's train of thought, Finn nudged the accelerator, spinning the forward thrusters and propelling them back toward the ledge. Descending until the bottom of the craft grazed the coral and sand, Finn shined the light. A streak penetrated beneath the fanned branch of coral, revealing the lobster, a crowd of its buddies, and a small open space beyond their shifting antennae.

Finn looked over at Alejandra just as a big smile formed on her face.

"I think it's time we took the drone for a spin," she said.

Deployable from the outside of the sub, Finn released an ROV, or remotely operated vehicle. With the manned submersible steady in its place, he took control of the drone, accelerating its small, sleek body away from its mothership. Behind the little craft, a yellow tether paid out from the submersible, and the line gave the drone over a thousand feet to play with.

He motored underneath the wide stretch of table coral and shined the light into the opening. Both Finn and Alejandra were able to watch via an onboard flatscreen as the hidden world came into view. When the spooked lobster cleared, the opening into a dark cave appeared.

"I do believe you've found Kidd's hiding place," Finn said, unable to contain his excitement.

"We found it," Alejandra said, patting him on the back. "Now, let's just hope he actually hid something in here."

Finn eased the small ROV through the opening, then up into the cave. A few pesky crabs and an irritated green eel watched as he motored the device deeper.

The jagged, growth-covered rock gave way to sleek, jutting walls of limestone the deeper they went.

As Finn weaved the tiny craft back and forth through the tunnel, Alejandra said, "How in the hell did Kidd find this place? Sucked into it during a storm? It's like something out of—"

"Treasure Island?" Finn said. "You know Robert Louis Stevenson supposedly got the idea for his book from Kidd, right? It's believed that Norman Island, just thirty miles southwest of here, is where Stevenson got his idea for the geography of his famous fictional island."

As Finn motored the drone, he noticed the current growing stronger, the waters of the narrow space sucking the craft deeper.

"I've never seen anything like this," Finn said, having to compensate with every maneuver to avoid bashing the vehicle against the rock.

"Imagine during a storm?" Alejandra said. "It's no wonder Kidd and his buddy were pulled into this thing."

The current didn't abate, forcing the ROV deeper into the cave until, after rounding a corner, the waters let up as the cave opened at a dead end.

"Tilt it back," Alejandra said, motioning toward the controls.

Finn did as she suggested, using the thrusters to angle their view of the cave. Overhead, they caught a clear glimpse of the dark surface.

The two glanced at each other, gave out an astonished gasp, then cheered.

"You getting this, Scott?" Finn said after a quick onboard celebration.

"Prettiest sight I've seen in a while," he replied. "You ascend for a better look?"

Finn piloted the craft up through the clear water, breaking the surface. The drone's lights beamed out from the water, illuminating an open space. They couldn't see any sign of human activity, but after scanning a full circle, they spotted a narrow passageway up through the rock.

Finn zoomed in on the opening. "I do believe we have ourselves a genuine pirate cave."

"Now, the only question is," Alejandra said, "how are we going to get in there?"

TWENTY-EIGHT

NIKOLAI REZNIKOV STRODE down the steps of his private jet and onto the tarmac of the Terrance B. International Airport. A man in a black suit and sunglasses opened the back door of an idling SUV, and the Russian plopped inside.

"Where to, boss?" the driver said.

Reznikov kept his eyes forward, his face stoic. "To the Paradise Bay Hotel."

The driver hit the gas, and Reznikov went back to his intense thoughts. He'd been stewing the entire flight back to the islands. The news of their failed attack in Scotland and the loss of his right-hand man had hit him hard. Boris had been fighting alongside him and protecting his life for years, and Reznikov knew it would've taken a highly trained killer to take him down.

Jason Wake is proving to be more difficult to deal with than I'd imagined. But he's crossed the line and will soon pay dearly for all that he's done.

"The governor has arrived, sir," the man in the passenger seat said.

"Tell him I will be there shortly."

When they arrived in Road Town, the capital of the BVI, the driver cruised them along Road Harbor, cutting through the bustling center of island life and marine activity in the archipelago. On the other side of the colorful, picturesque seaside town, the driver pulled into the entrance of a bright orange resort nestled between green hills and the waterfront.

The back door opened, and Reznikov sauntered inside, heading straight for the elevator. Entering his room on the top floor, he spotted a thin Englishman standing near the sliding glass door to the balcony.

"You're late, Nikolai," the Englishman said as he adjusted the cuffs of his slim-fitted suit.

"I had . . . important matters to attend to."

David Calvert stuck out his chest and pressed his hands to his hips, but his façade crumbled with one cold look by the Russian. "Right," Calvert said. "Well, things aren't looking good. I believe the time has come for us to pursue other courses of action."

Reznikov narrowed his gaze. "You got something you want to tell me?"

Calvert sighed. "It's time to end this. You haven't followed through on your end of the deal."

"The treasure's there. It's within my grasp, and you want to quit now?"

"*Our* grasp. And what makes you think you can find it? Your men have been blowing up the reef for weeks with nothing to show for it."

"You let me handle that."

Calvert grabbed a glass of brandy from the table in front of him and took a slow sip. "I'm tired of your empty promises, and I'm beyond tired of covering for you. It's time to admit that this isn't working. We need to scratch this whole thing before it's too late."

Reznikov strode to the window and gazed out over the seaside harbor. "Do you have any idea how tall this building is?"

"How the hell should I know?"

"We're on the seventh floor," Reznikov said, rubbing his chin. "At roughly just over four meters per floor, that means approximately thirty meters—give or take."

"What the hell is your point, Nikolai?"

The Russian nodded at one of his guards. In a blink, two men grabbed the governor from behind and forced him toward Reznikov.

Calvert lost control of his drink, and the glass cracked on the tile floor. "Hey, what the hell is this?"

Reznikov answered only by sliding open the door at his back and stepping out onto the balcony. His two men followed, hauling the politician out on the deck.

"Thirty meters." Reznikov peered over the railing at the rocky shoreline. "That's going to be very painful for you."

He gave his men another nod, then stepped aside as they hoisted Calvert off his feet and suspended him by his ankles over nothing but open air.

"What the hell!" Calvert gasped, his eyes bulging as he focused on the ground far below.

"You were saying?" Reznikov said.

"I . . . I . . ." The governor went into a panic, heaving for air.

"You will do as I say," Reznikov stated. "You will continue with the plan."

The politician nodded rapidly as his pale face turned crimson.

"Say it." Reznikov grabbed him by his shirt collar. "Say it . . . now."

"I will do as you say," Calvert wheezed. "I will do as you say, and we'll continue with the plan."

Reznikov smiled, then let go. "And you will never doubt me again."

"I will never doubt you again. Please . . . I will do whatever you want."

Reznikov enjoyed watching the coward plead for his life. Once he felt he'd made his point, he stepped back and motioned to his guards. The two henchmen lifted Calvert back over the railing, then dropped him onto the hard deck.

Reznikov gave Calvert only seconds to catch his breath before gripping him by his collar and yanking him to his feet.

"Pull yourself together," Reznikov spat, then straightened the guy's shirt. He gripped Calvert by the back of his neck and looked him dead in the eye. "Now, you will be standing by when I call on you. You will need to act quickly, and your men will need to be ready. I can't afford any mistakes. And if I catch even a whiff of your backing out . . ." Reznikov scowled over the balcony. "Well, let's just say there are limits to my patience, and you're treading on the fringes."

Calvert swallowed hard. "My men and I will be ready. When you make the call, we will be there, and we will do whatever you need."

Reznikov smiled and patted the Englishman on the back. He strode back inside, leaving the shell-shocked governor paralyzed on the balcony.

Once back in the suv, Reznikov ordered his driver to take them to the downtown marina.

"The trucks are in the warehouse near the ferry terminal," one of his men said.

"Have the men bring the vehicles to Anegada, and keep them hidden for now. There they will stand by until our contact on the inside gives us the green light."

"And . . . what if they don't follow through?"

"They will," Reznikov spat. "I've made sure of that."

For Reznikov, there was no plan B. The Russian criminal was drowning in debt, and if he couldn't come up with a hefty amount of cash—and fast—everything he owned would be taken away from him. He'd be left with nothing and publicly disgraced.

Reznikov couldn't fathom that. He couldn't allow failure to overtake them, no matter how many men he lost or how many innocent lives it took.

Kidd's treasure will be mine, he thought. *And anyone who stands in my way will die.*

TWENTY-NINE

JASON STRODE ALONG the pristine northeastern shoreline, pushing a four-wheeled device over the untouched sandy beach toward Pelican Point. The GPR, or ground-penetrating radar unit, looked like a black and red push lawn mower with rubber tires and an LCD screen on the handlebars.

After rolling over a quarter mile of brilliant white sand, he stopped, wiped the sweat from his brow, and studied the digital display.

"Anything?" Charlotte said from just up the beach.

"Nothing yet."

Jason recalibrated the GPR, making sure it was working correctly. It was his first time using this technology, so the grainy image and controls were new to him, aside from the quick tutorial Finn had given. The advanced machine used pulses of sound waves to detect subsurface objects, and most importantly to Jason, voids.

Resetting the device, Jason adjusted the gain until a cluster of wavy gray lines filled the top of the screen. Much like airborne radar, the sound pulses emitted are reflected and used to form a two-dimensional image.

Once ready, Jason gripped the handlebars and continued to push the machine. Based on Kidd's journal, the cave extended from the reef line to the shore. Scanning along the beach, they were hoping to discover the pocket of open air where the cave reached the island.

It was just after noon. The two had arrived in Tortola earlier that day after catching a connecting flight in Miami. After being picked up and briefed on the team's progress aboard the *Valiant*, they'd both been eager to dive into the task of discovering a way to enter into the cave. Jason was just about to continue his path along the surf when his phone buzzed in his pocket.

"Just got back from the dive," Finn said after Jason answered. "Still no luck."

"You tried without the gear?"

"Yeah, I removed the BCD and tried to shimmy in like John Chatterton while he was exploring the lost U-boat off New Jersey. It's still way too snug. And we searched over every inch of the reef, and that's the only opening we could find. The only way anyone's getting in that gap is by blasting away the reef."

"Well, we'll just have to count on the other entrance," Jason said. "Keep your eyes peeled. We'll let you know if we pick up anything with the radar."

They ended the call, and Jason gripped the device and continued his slow trek along the beach, keeping a watchful eye on the screen. It was a beautiful Caribbean day—eighty degrees, thin patches of clouds against a crisp blue sky, a welcomed ocean breeze, and a never-ending sea of aqua surrounding them. Crashing waves rumbled over the distant reefs and lapped against the picturesque coast.

Aside from birds, Jason and Charlotte were the only life for miles. They enjoyed the quiet and the gentle sounds of palm fronds in the ocean breeze. The scene, combined with the excitement of having discovered Kidd's cave in the reef, gave Jason a heightened sense of anticipation, but the potential threat of coming danger still weighed heavily on their minds. They'd taken down Boris Konstantine, yes, but Reznikov wouldn't give up that easy. They were both sure of that.

After pushing the device another quarter mile and not seeing any discrepancies indicating underground cavities, Jason stopped and examined the machine again.

"You think there's something wrong with it?" Charlotte asked. "Based on the description in Kidd's journal, we should've seen the cave by now."

"Maybe," Jason said, kneeling down and playing with a few buttons. "I'll call Finn. He's the mechanical guy."

"Don't sell yourself short. You were pretty mechanical when you hotwired that car back in Scotland."

"Stripping wires and programming an advanced piece of survey equipment are two very different things."

Jason pulled his phone out again and strode toward the surf. He peered out over the water, shielding the sun from his eyes as he observed the *Valiant* anchored a mile offshore. He called Finn back while picking up a few rocks and tossing them into the water. After Finn let him know that he'd be on his way in fifteen, Jason pocketed the phone and then noticed something glistening in the shallows. Kneeling down, he picked up a small conch shell. Knowing that in some cultures, the shell was a sign of good luck, he examined the brown and white exterior and pink interior for a moment before tossing the occupied shell into the water.

Charlotte had continued pushing the device along the same line, so he chuckled and strode toward her. "The woman doesn't have a shortage of optimism," he whispered to himself. "I'll give her that."

Just as he approached, she froze, her eyes glued on the screen.

"Finn will be on his way soon," Jason said. "Maybe he can—"

"I found it!" she exclaimed, leaning in closer to the display.

Jason rapidly closed the distance, and as he fixated on the screen, he saw a pocket of open space roughly ten feet beneath them. Jason reasoned that the cavity was over six feet tall. As they moved the device, they saw that it extended both inland and out to the sea.

Jason embraced Charlotte, a wave of excitement and relief rushing over him.

"All it took was a woman's touch," she said, patting the machine.

"Apparently. Feel free to take over."

With Charlotte pushing the GPR unit, they followed the cave for thirty feet, then reached the end of the sand.

"It keeps going," she said.

In front of them was a densely packed forest of mangroves that hugged the beach in both directions. Leaving the machine for the time being, Jason grabbed his gear bag, and the two climbed up through the tangle of trees, slowly navigating their way to Budrock Pond on the other side of the foliage. Roughly a mile long and a thousand feet wide, the pool of brackish water was one of four ponds that combined to cover over a quarter of the island. The two gazed out over the water, eyeing a flock of flamingoes wading on the opposite side.

"Kidd escaped by swimming out into a lake," Charlotte said, recounting the journal entry.

They climbed down a bank, pushing their way through thick branches before reaching the shore. The pond was mostly shallow, but to their left was a dark, murky spot that was clearly much deeper. Jason threw off his shirt, grabbed a dive mask from his bag, and dipped into the pond.

"I wonder how low snorkeling the famous brackish ponds is on Anegada's list of popular tourist attractions," Charlotte said.

Jason chuckled. "I'm banking on it being near the bottom."

He slipped on his mask, threw Charlotte a thumbs-up, then dropped beneath the surface. What little visibility there was quickly vanished as he descended. As careful as Jason was not to disturb the sediment, his movements churned up small clouds of muck in the water as he felt his way toward the center of the pool.

It quickly got too deep for him to touch, so he did a slow and smooth duck dive, then kicked for the bottom. After what felt like an eternity of swimming in the haze of stagnate water, he touched the mushy bottom. Shifting his body around, he planted his feet into the muddy lake floor and felt along the rocky edge of the pond. The rough surface was infested by tangles of roots, so the going was slow. After spending nearly two minutes beneath the surface, he felt his lungs begin to throb, and he ascended.

"Any sign of an opening?" Charlotte asked as Jason caught his breath.

"No sign of anything." He pointed toward his gear bag. "You mind tossing me my dive light?"

She rummaged through the bag, grabbed the waterproof flashlight, and gave it a toss.

After snatching it, Jason flipped on the light. "Round two." He adjusted the beam's intensity, sucked in a deep breath, and descended back into the abyss.

When he reached the bottom and felt around the rock, he couldn't believe how excited he was. The idea that they were closing in on a pirate treasure that had been hidden by one of the most famous buccaneers to ever set sail filled him with a romantic breed of excitement he couldn't describe. He'd been feeling it all day, though in reality, the suspense had been growing ever since Charlotte told him about the Captain Kidd legend.

Suddenly, Jason's hand grazed over a pointed edge in the rock face, snagging him from his thoughts. So far, everything he'd touched had been smooth. It was the right angle that caught him off guard.

Shifting closer, Jason shined the light while clearing away the gunk with his free hand. His lungs began to throb again, reminding him that he was human and needed oxygen to live. Unable to surface without seeing what it was, Jason continued scraping away the dirt with his fingers and trying to figure out what he'd found.

He gripped an edge of mud and clay and tore it off, a foggy cloud of dirt bursting around him. As it began to clear, a surge of euphoria rushed through his body when he realized that what he'd touched wasn't rock at all—it was brick.

THIRTY

JASON BROKE THE surface, forcing out the remaining air from his lungs and inhaling a series of deep breaths.

Charlotte stood on the shore, looking over a GPS image on a tablet. "You all right?"

Jason gave her the okay signal. He'd been close to blacking out, having flirted with the limit of his breath-holding ability, but he didn't care. A broad smile formed on his face.

Charlotte tilted her head and leaned forward in anticipation. "You find the cave?"

Jason shook his head. "No. Looks like somebody blocked it off. And I'm willing to bet that our notorious pirate friend might be to blame."

She looked at him, confused.

"Come on in," Jason said. "I'll show you."

Charlotte removed her shorts and tank top, revealing a purple one-piece swimsuit she'd picked up in Tortola. She was in great shape and pretty, but it was her mind and quick wit that Jason was most attracted to. The two dove down, and Jason showed her the brick wall.

When they surfaced and Charlotte expressed her excitement at their find, Jason splashed to the shore and called Finn. "Hey, you still on the *Valiant*?"

"Just about to shove off. What's up?"

"Do me a favor and bring two sets of dive gear and more underwater flashlights when you come . . . and a sledgehammer."

Scott, Finn, and Alejandra motored the RHIB onto the beach five minutes later. After dragging the craft away from the surf, Jason and Charlotte helped them unload the gear. They lugged it all through the mangroves and settled onto a patch of grass just up from the pond.

Excited to see what was on the other side of the brick wall, Jason quickly donned a wetsuit and a full set of scuba gear. Wading into the water with a sledgehammer in his hands, he gave the team a thumbs-up before dropping down into the murky pool. Venting all the air from his BCD, he swiftly reached the bottom and planted his feet into the muddy lake floor. He inspected the brick wall, utilizing a flashlight attached to his mask.

The rest of the group were anxiously standing above, watching through a camera attached to Jason's mask and communicating with him via the built-in radio. Jason grazed his left hand along the partly crumbling brick. It didn't take a thorough inspection to see that it was well over a hundred years old. The group had concluded that after hiding his treasure, Kidd decided to block off the underwater entrance into the cave to keep his loot hidden. His ploy had worked even better than the pirate could've imagined, keeping the cave, and whatever lay inside it, locked away from the eyes and minds of the human race for hundreds of years.

Jason concentrated on a brick near the middle of the wall, then reared back the twenty-pound steel head. Flexing his muscles, he swung the sledge as fast as he could through the water and struck the brick. If the wall was affected by the blow, it didn't show it. The metal chipped a small piece of brick but did little to dislodge any of the blocks.

"This may take a while," Jason said.

With the resistance of the water substantially slowing his motion, Jason attacked the wall again and again, pounding it ferociously. After twenty strikes of the mallet, one of the bricks loosened. Three more blows and the brick fell free, revealing a dark void beyond it. Jason lowered the sledgehammer and shined his light into the small opening. Beyond the wall, he saw a cave that cut deep into the rock, growing in size as it went.

Excited by what they'd found, and energized by the newfound weak point in the wall, Jason grabbed his weapon of choice and went back to work, beating away the bricks until there was a space big enough to fit through. His muscles burning from the exertion, Jason set the hammer aside and focused on the opening.

Charlotte donned a second set of dive gear, descended, and moved in beside him.

"Guess I don't need to hit the gym today," Jason said. Shining his light through the newly formed hole in the brick wall, he patted Charlotte on the back. "What do you say? You ready to walk in Kidd's footsteps?"

The archeologist grinned behind her mask. "You have no idea."

Wanting to make sure it was safe, Jason finned in first, keeping his movements slow and steady. In all likelihood, no one had entered that cave in hundreds of years, so they had no way of knowing how stable or unstable it was.

Barely able to fit through the initial section of the cave, they soon rounded a corner, and the cave opened up. Finning another twenty yards, Jason shined his light skyward and saw the surface ten feet above.

"The pool described in Kidd's journal," Charlotte said, shining her light along the top of the water until it illuminated the shallow end of the underground body of water.

Jason discharged air from his tank into his BCD, then kicked smoothly for the surface. The two broke out from the water, side by side, and pulled off their masks. The cave was bigger than they'd imagined—easily over ten feet tall and sixty feet long. Water covered most of it, but along the far wall was a patch of dry land, along with an opening into a dark passageway.

"If that isn't a good sign, I don't know what is," Charlotte said. She illuminated a faded image of a skull and crossbones, the famous symbol found on Jolly Roger pirate flags.

"And that sure isn't man-made," Jason said, pointing at a stone table with old chains resting at its base.

Unable to contain their excitement, the two laughed and embraced before slogging out of the water. After removing their gear, they scanned the cave once more before continuing down the passageway.

"The question I keep asking myself," Charlotte said, "is how did Kidd and his men manage to hide treasure down here? I mean, they supposedly carried treasures all the way through that tunnel, underwater, with no modern equipment."

"You're underestimating mankind," Jason said. "People are capable of incredible things and have been since the first humans. Just think of the pyramids, or the Roman Colosseum, or the Great Wall of China. If Kidd wanted to hide his treasure here, a man of his intelligence and drive would find a way to make it happen."

They pressed onward, twisting and turning and admiring more markings on the walls. With each step, Jason's anticipation grew. Navigating around a series of bends in the cave and a dislodged boulder, they saw that the passageway opened up again. As they climbed through the opening and into the cavity, the beams of their flashlights sparkled back at them.

Jason and Charlotte gasped as they laid eyes on old chests overflowing with gold and silver. Both stunned speechless, they stood in awe of the treasures before them—a mountain of gold and silver and jewels that had been lost to the tides of time.

Shaking from the trance the extraordinary sight had induced, they laughed and let out a chorus of triumphant cheers. Jason lifted Charlotte off the ground as tears streaked down the archeologist's face. After spinning her around twice, he set her back down, and the two continued to chuckle as they caught their breath.

It wasn't the wealth that excited Charlotte; it was the fact that a legend she'd believed in for years was real—that Kidd had been telling the truth and that her gut had been right. After letting go of each other, the two sprang toward the treasure, eagerly examining every inch of it.

Charlotte ran her hands over one of the chests. "It says 'Santa Isabella.' These chests were on a Spanish galleon that disappeared in the late seventeenth century on its way to Spain from Mexico. Must've struck the reef in a storm."

Jason moved across the cave to a second pile. Searching the chests, he found one with a placard like the other. "Defiance," he said, reading it aloud. "I think it must be English." When he didn't get a reply, he turned to see Charlotte standing in the middle of the cave, riffling through her front pocket.

"Looks like we might have the riches from multiple wrecks here," Jason added. "Given the stories of all the ships that Horseshoe Reef has claimed over the years, I'm not surprised."

Jason grabbed his radio. He held the talk button down, eager to relay what they'd found, but heard only thick static blaring through the speaker.

"Maybe we should head back," Charlotte said.

Jason shook his head. "What do you mean? We just got here. You don't want to look over the rest of it?"

"I think we should head back." She hustled across the cave and grabbed Jason by the arm.

After taking a few strides, Jason stopped her. "You've been waiting your whole life to find this treasure, and now—"

"Jason," she said, tearing up again. "You don't understand. I . . . I have to—"

Charlotte's words were interrupted by a violent rumble that erupted from overhead and shook the cave.

THIRTY-ONE

SCOTT, ALEJANDRA, AND Finn stood along the edge of the pond, anticipation brewing as they stared at the tablet displaying Jason's mask cam. The trio watched eagerly as Jason broke apart piece after piece of the brick wall. Once the opening was large enough, he set the hammer aside and finned into the cave. After turning left and then right, the image displayed a large cavity. Then, up ahead, they saw the surface illuminated by the light.

The three let out a cheer, then Scott grabbed the radio.

"Looks like we've got a winner, kid," he exclaimed. His voice was cut off by the sound of static. "Wake, you there?"

"No signal?" Alejandra said.

Finn grabbed the radio and looked it over. "That's strange. I calibrated it for the occasion myself. It's set to a low frequency and should have no trouble communicating underground."

They tried again and again to get ahold of them but got nothing. Then the camera feed vanished, as well.

Finn shook his head. "Must be some kind of technical issue. Of course it would happen right now, of all times."

Just as the words left Finn's lips, Scott's sat phone buzzed in his pocket. For a moment, he was hopeful it might be Jase—that he'd brought his phone and the signal was able to make it. But as he pulled it out and glanced at the screen, he saw that it was from the radar tech aboard the *Valiant*.

"There's a police boat heading your way, boss," the man said in a Southern accent. "At first, I thought they were just surveying the area, but it's clear that they're heading straight for the beach."

Scott lowered the phone and heard the sound of outboard motors in the distance. "It's just the police," he said, seeing the reaction on Finn and Alejandra's faces. "I'll take care of it. You two stay here in case they come back up. And see if you can get that radio to work." He trudged off through the thick tangles of trees.

Scott reached the beach just as an aluminum-hulled Royal Police boat splashed onto the sand, and three men in uniforms hopped out just beside their RHIB. As the men closed in on Scott, they each grabbed a sidearm and aimed it at him.

Scott threw his hands in the air. "Whoa, easy!" His pistol was tucked into the back of his waistband, and the former Special Forces commander could snatch it and engage the men in the blink of an eye, but they were law enforcement, and he had no intention of taking them on.

"We're not the enemy here," Scott continued as they closed in on him. "We're with Ocean Revival, and we're—"

"On the ground, now!" one of them shouted.

"My name is Scott Cooper." He kept his voice loud but composed. The last thing he wanted was to spook a trigger-happy officer. "We have permission from the BVI's Ninth District Representative to be here."

"We'll see about that," another said. "But we have explicit orders to keep these waters safe. And with all of the illegal activity over the past month, you and your operation are suspect, Mr. Cooper."

"If you'd let me show you my credentials, I can prove that we have permission to be here."

The officer waved him off. "I'm not interested in that right now. I have orders to keep this beach clear, and that's what we're gonna do." Seeing Finn and Alejandra approach, the guy ordered the two others to bring them over at gunpoint. The policeman sighed. "Look, if this is all just a big misunderstanding, we'll get it cleared up quickly. But my orders are clear, and they've come straight from the governor."

"David Calvert?" Scott noted the officer's collar device and name tag. "Sergeant Graham, with all due respect, you need to listen to me here."

"The governor is aboard now," Graham said, pointing toward a large patrol boat just offshore. "He requests your presence. If this is a misunderstanding, I'm sure you'll work it out."

Seeing that they had no choice but to play ball, Scott turned to the others as he was led toward the police boat.

Finn bit his lip. "What about Jase and Charlotte?"

"We'll fix this up quickly," Scott said. "They'll be fine."

Finn and Alejandra were forced to board the RHIB and motor back to the *Valiant*, where they were to stay put until further instruction.

"This way, sir," Graham said, motioning Scott toward the boat.

Scott climbed aboard, and the captain fired up the outboards, bouncing them over the surf and heading for the sixty-foot police boat, which was floating roughly half a mile from the *Valiant*. Motoring up along the port side of the cabin cruiser, Scott was offered help across the gap, but he conquered it with ease.

"He up on the bow?" Scott said, striding toward the forward section of the sixty-foot boat.

Graham nodded, barely able to keep up with Scott, who wanted to handle the misunderstanding as quickly as possible—to get in and out and get their show back on the road. Scott had been dealing with government, both big and small, for years. He knew as well as anyone how simple misunderstandings can rack up unnecessary hours and funds to a project.

A high-pitched male voice called out to Scott as he hustled around the cockpit.

"Welcome aboard, Mr. Cooper."

Scott recognized the voice. David Calvert was standing near the bow rail with his hands in his pockets.

"I thought the local district representative oversaw this island," Scott said, striding toward the British diplomat.

"Sorry to disappoint, but I'm handling this situation now."

Scott had hoped to avoid working with Calvert, preferring the local islander politicians.

"Jackie gave us permission to search here," Scott said, referring to the district representative. "I'm sure she briefed you on what we're up to and who we're trying to prevent from getting their hands on this find."

The pale, skinny man raised his eyebrows. "So, you have found it, I presume?"

"Not yet."

Calvert nodded. "I see. Well, yes, Miss Frazer has informed me that she's given you her approval. But . . . you are a politician, Mr. Cooper, so I know you will understand."

"Understand what?"

The man smiled. "That sometimes concessions must be made. Partnerships must be formed that appear negative when viewed at face value, but in reality, they offer the greatest benefit for the people I represent."

The sounds of distant engines caught Scott's attention, and he moved forward and gazed out toward the shore of Anegada. Three off-road trucks were rumbling down the beach.

Scott turned back to the governor. "What are you doing, Calvert?"

The smug politician held up his hands. "I'm only doing what I believe is best for my people."

"You mean for your bank account."

The two officers at Scott's back crept in closer. "Don't be so naïve, Mr. Cooper. A man such as yourself is well versed in the ways of the world."

The governor gave a slight nod, and the two officers pounced, snatching Scott at the wrists. He broke free and spun around in a blink. Sweeping a leg, he knocked one of the guys on his butt while lunging toward the second and ramming him to the deck. A quick knee and a kick, and both men were incapacitated. It had taken all of two seconds for Scott to take them down, but as he turned and faced Calvert again, he realized that the barrels of three rifles were aimed straight at him.

Calvert smiled. "You've got some serious explaining to do, Mr. Cooper." The governor shifted his attention to the officers. "Sergeant, he is to be held in captivity and charged with assaulting royal officers, violation of regulatory laws, and the solicitation of a bribe to a public official." He shot Scott a cocky smile. "Take him away."

Graham nodded, and his men closed in and cuffed Scott's wrists behind his back. Scott took one more look at Calvert before his attention was suddenly drawn to the sound of automatic gunfire echoing from the island's shoreline. He struggled to catch a look at the commotion, and before he homed in on the source of the gunfire, Calvert relieved one of the officers of his rifle and bashed the stock into Scott's head.

THIRTY-TWO

FINN STARED INTENTLY through a pair of long-range binoculars, focusing on the bow of the Royal Police patrol boat.

"How's it going?" Alejandra asked.

The two were standing along the port gunwale on the main deck of the *Valiant*, having just reached topside after hustling from the RHIB deployment room.

Finn shrugged, then lowered the binos and handed them to Alejandra. "Hard to tell from this far off."

She grabbed them and peeped through the lenses.

"But the timing sure is troubling," he continued. "Think about it. Right when we enter the cave, these guys swoop in."

"What are you saying?"

"Just that I'm not usually prone to believing in coincidences."

"Me, neither."

After watching the conversation between Scott and the BVI's governor on the bow of the boat closely for a minute, Alejandra perked up as she heard engines growing far off in the distance.

"Sounds like diesels," Finn said. He pointed toward the shore. "Over there."

Alejandra turned to face the faraway rumbles and adjusted the focus. "There's three of them. Big rigs. And they're moving fast." She lowered the binos and shot Finn a skeptical gaze. "Now we're past coincidences. Something's going on here." She squinted back toward the bow of the patrol boat. "Something's—"

Two of the officers closed in behind Scott, and in a blur of movement, their leader sent the two men to the deck. But more took their place, and they aimed their rifles straight at Scott.

"Definitely not a coincidence," Alejandra said. "We need to move now!"

The two notified the rest of the crew that they were under attack, then scrambled down into the RHIB deployment room. Swiftly opening the stern door, Finn geared up the conveyer belt system while Alejandra climbed into the boat.

"What exactly is the plan here?" Finn said as he motored them away from the *Valiant*. "We can't just attack a police boat."

"We're not going for the boat," she replied, yelling over the wind. "We need to help Jase and Charlotte."

Finn turned toward the beach, bouncing over wave after wave as they rushed toward the three trucks. They didn't know how many there were or how much firepower they had, and they prepared themselves for the worst. As if to answer the question, the three trucks stopped near where Jason had discovered the cave using the ground-penetrating radar earlier that day. Men with guns hopped out of the vehicles, striding toward the surf and taking aim toward Alejandra and Finn.

"Finn!" Alejandra called out, pointing toward the beach.

The Venezuelan reacted quickly, shifting their course by abruptly turning the helm to starboard. The small craft nearly flipped as it cut sharply, bouncing high over the waves and accelerating north.

Without warning, the men on the beach opened fire. Before the RHIB could motor around the point, two rounds struck the port pontoon. A loud *pop* was followed by a hiss as air rushed out from the compartment. The rapid loss of buoyancy caused the craft to lurch, and before Finn could ease back their speed, they flipped and were tossed into the water.

THIRTY-THREE

NIKOLAI REZNIKOV SAT in the passenger seat of the off-road pickup as it rumbled along the dirt road.

"The police are clearing the scene now," a man said from the back seat after lowering his phone.

"How many were there?" Reznikov said.

"Three, including Mr. Cooper."

Reznikov smiled. That meant Wake would still be there. After all the American had done over the past week, he wanted nothing more than to see Wake's face as his whole world collapsed around him.

"Take us to the beach," Reznikov said. He glanced over his shoulder toward the bed of the truck. "We have a package that needs to be delivered."

His men smiled.

The driver reached the end of the road, then cut through a thin cluster of trees and burst out onto the beach. The two other trucks followed right behind as they roared over the sand, flying southeast. Five minutes later, they rounded a bend in the shoreline. Reznikov held up a GPS unit that displayed their position on the island. Up ahead, a red dot indicated the coordinates of their destination.

"Just up the beach another quarter mile," he said.

The driver continued at the armada's blistering pace, flying over the beach at over forty miles per hour. Peering out through the passenger window, Reznikov spotted a black boat motoring toward them, heading from the direction of the research vessel anchored offshore.

Brave but stupid, he thought as he shook his head.

He turned to the guy in the back seat. "Looks like we have company. Tell your men to prepare for target practice."

The man smiled and relayed the message to the two other trucks. Just as the tires braked them to a stop at their destination, a cluster of men hopped out, bolted toward the surf, and raised their weapons.

"Bring them down!" Reznikov spat as he slid out from his seat.

His men didn't hesitate. Three of them opened fire, the loud pops filling the air as they sent rounds flying toward the RHIB. The boat turned sharply, bullets puncturing its hull just before it reached the point. The craft flipped, crashing as it disappeared from view beyond the jutting stretch of beach.

Reznikov and his men let out chuckles, relishing the sad attempt their adversaries had made.

"Mr. Cooper has been detained aboard the patrol boat," one of Reznikov's men said.

The Russian inhaled a deep breath of ocean air and closed his eyes. "You smell that, men? *That* is the smell of victory."

Reznikov strode along the sand while holding his GPS, then stopped when he reached the identified location. "Now that they've been removed, it's time to deal with the remaining pests." With the rage from hearing of Boris's death still burning hot within him, Reznikov pointed at the sand. "Put the packages in place."

Three of his men rushed to the back of a truck, grabbed black duffel bags, and stacked them in a pyramid on the beach. Once they were all set, they climbed back into the trucks and drove a hundred yards from the pile.

After he was handed the remote, Reznikov stared intently through the windshield at the stack of bags, then flicked the switch.

THIRTY-FOUR

THE EXPLOSION WAS so powerful and sudden that it knocked Jason and Charlotte to the ground. Jason grabbed hold of her in the chaos and tried to take the brunt of the landing with everything he had, but in the rumbling darkness, he couldn't see anything as they rolled and the earth crumbled apart around them.

The roof of the cave was blasted to pieces, and stones and shards rained down upon them, rumbling to the earth and shaking the cave like a powerful earthquake. The two slammed against a wall, then their bodies contorted to wedge down a passageway that led to the ocean.

As the rocks and dust settled, Jason was amazed he was still breathing, let alone in one piece. His body ached from the fall, and his ears rang from the explosion, but he was still alive and still able to move his body.

"Charlotte?" He struggled to get her name out as he felt movement beside him. He coughed up dust, then sucked in a breath. "Are you all right?" He shuffled in closer, then leaned over her face.

She was covered in dirt, and her clothes were tattered, but she was still breathing. With light bleeding down from the newly formed opening at the top of the cave, Jason saw her pale face and tears streaking down her cheeks.

"Charlotte, what's wrong?" Jason said, searching over her body. "Are you hurt?"

"I'm sorry, Jason." She slowly reached up and laid a trembling hand on his cheek. "I'm so sorry."

Voices sounded from overhead, and Jason forced himself onto a knee. Even from far off and muffled from the cave, he recognized the strong, poisonous Russian accent—a menacing voice that hurt his ears. Nikolai Reznikov.

How in the hell did he find us? Jason thought. *And where are Scott, Alejandra, and Finn?*

He shook himself from his thoughts. There was no time to question how or why they'd fallen into the bleak predicament. What mattered was how they handled it, and Jason knew their only way out was to run—to get out of there as fast as they could and reevaluate. He didn't know how many men Reznikov had, but neither he nor Charlotte were armed, and it wouldn't take a crack shot to gun them down in that confining cave.

Jason wrapped his arms around a still-stunned Charlotte, trying to will her to her feet.

"Hey, we need to move. They'll be down here any second." Finally, she gained some strength, and they both struggled to their feet. "Come on," Jason said, motioning toward the passageway.

He started to move, but Charlotte remained stoic.

"Jason," she said, pulling him back.

"What are you doing? We can't take on all these guys. We—" Jason froze, staring deep into Charlotte's eyes. "You. . . ."

Rivers of tears streaked down her face, and she began to shake.

Jason's mouth fell open, and he shook his head, completely taken aback by what was happening. "How . . . how could you?"

"I'm sorry, Jason." Hearing a loud grinding noise and low voices barking overhead, Charlotte grabbed Jason by the arm and pointed down the dark passageway. "You go without me. There's still time if you hurry."

"But what about you? They'll kill you."

"We won't kill her, Mr. Wake," Reznikov said as a metal platform lowered him and three of his goons into the cave.

Jason spun around and glared at the group.

The corrupt Russian held his ivory cane in one hand and a glistening Makarov .45-caliber pistol in the other, the barrel aimed straight at Jason. Three others held submachine guns and kept them locked on Jason.

When the platform reached the bottom and the machine overhead stopped humming, Reznikov stepped out with an evil, satisfied smile on his face. "That's part of the deal, isn't it, Miss Murchison? You get to walk away unharmed."

"I'm sorry, Jason," Charlotte said again. "I had no choice."

"She was playing you all along, Wake." He shook his head, then wiped his lips. "And now . . . now she's led us straight to Kidd's treasure." He looked around the cave at the stacks of chests and the gold spilling out around him. "With this great treasure and the local politicians in my pocket, I'll have no trouble taking over this island. If I could, I would've simply wiped out the native population here like the unapologetic conquerors of old. But sadly, I am forced to handle the situation more humanely. And with more cunning."

"Where's Scott and the others?" Jason said, unable to even look at Charlotte.

Reznikov smiled. "Always worried about other people, aren't you, Wake? Mr. Cooper is alive, for now, but I can't speak for your other friends."

Jason clenched his jaw.

"You know, I must admit that I underestimated you," the Russian continued. "I imagined you'd be nothing more than a nuisance when you made your sudden, dramatic appearance back in Italy, but you managed to take down my best man. And for that, I cannot offer you any form of mercy." With the gun still aimed at Jason, he turned to Charlotte. "Get in, Miss Murchison. Your job here is done."

Charlotte continued apologizing to Jason, but he didn't reply or look her way.

"Today, Miss Murchison," Reznikov snarled.

She staggered across the rocky ground, and when she reached Reznikov, he grabbed her by the arm and yanked her onto the platform.

With the three other guns still aimed at Jason, Reznikov sauntered toward the American while sliding down the magazine from his Makarov and removing a high-caliber round.

"Mr. Wake, you know I am an avid hunter. Once, while on a hunt for grizzlies in your Rocky Mountains, I took down a twelve-hundred-pound beast with this very firearm. One might not suspect it to be so potent"—he held the round up to Jason, the copper jacket reflecting the sunlight bleeding down into the cavern—"but let me assure you, it will blast a hole through your chest six inches wide and hurl your guts all over this cave when I pull the trigger." He inserted the cartridge back into the magazine, then jammed the clip into his pistol.

"If you're trying to scare me, Nik, it won't work," Jason said, pushing his shoulders back and sticking his chest out. "Nothing you do will, because inside, I know you're nothing more than an old, miserable coward. And no matter what happens or what you do or how many people you screw over or murder, that will never change."

Reznikov licked the left side of his lip, his face scrunching up. He turned over his shoulder and ordered his men to begin loading up the treasure. One of the men kept his aim on Jason while the others stowed their weapons over their backs with the straps, then began heaving the chests onto the metal structure.

Reznikov aimed his weapon at Jason, savoring the anticipation of the moment as the first load of treasure was hauled up. Charlotte stared at Jason and shook her head while pressing a hand to her heart as the platform trembled and lifted her up out of sight.

Jason didn't know how Reznikov had manipulated her into joining his scheme or how long she'd been in on it. But none of that mattered. All that mattered was getting the hell out of there.

"I can already see it now," Reznikov said. "After squandering his fortune, the only son of Richard Wake tries to steal treasure from poor islanders. It'll make quite the story. I'm going to enjoy pinning this on you, Wake." He stepped closer and chuckled. "Like I said . . . I always win."

Reznikov narrowed his gaze, his finger flexing on the trigger.

Jason's mind ran wild. The clock was winding down, and he knew that any moment the sinister Russian would pull the trigger, closing the curtain on his life.

An eruption of gunfire blared out from overhead. Reznikov flinched, then angled his head skyward.

Knowing it was his only opportunity, Jason hurled his body down the passageway, vanishing into the darkness and twisting just as Reznikov snapped his head back.

The Russian pulled the trigger of his Makarov, shaking the cave to life as the round burst from the chamber and tore through the air. Jason heard the bullet zip by just overhead as he landed and forced his body to roll out of view. Once around the corner of jutting rock, he crawled, sprang to his feet, and took off with everything he had.

"Go get him!" Reznikov yelled to his men. "I want his body filled with bullets . . . on sight!"

Jason's heart pounded in his chest as he stumbled his way through the dark cave. Moments later, it turned pitch black, forcing him to feel his way along.

"You can't run, Wake!" Reznikov hollered through the cave. "There's nowhere to go!"

His words burned into Jason's mind as he banged his knees and hands against the rock with every turn. The sound of shuffling feet and voices reverberated down the cave at his back, and his pursuers' flash-lights danced like headlights in the distance, giving him a gut-wrenching reminder that they were right on his heels.

The mad Russian's right, Jason thought. *There's nowhere to run.*

He shoved the thoughts from his mind. He had no choice but to press on. With Reznikov's thugs bearing down on him, he was dead if he stayed put, so he had no choice but to go for it.

After what felt like an eternity winding through the pitch black with his pursuers on his heels, he reached a large chamber. His mind flashed to the journal entry he'd read dozens of times since first laying eyes on the text back in Scotland. Kidd and his companion had been sucked in to an underwater cave and were eventually tossed into a large cavity.

Sure enough, after traversing the space, his feet splashed into the water. Unable to stop himself, he slipped down the smooth rock and sloshed into the ocean.

Finn and Alejandra had only been able to enter the cave with the drone. It was too tight for the small Venezuelan to fit through, even without gear on. The facts didn't escape him, but with the two men charging into view with their weapons raised and his options limited to one, Jason took in a deep breath he knew would likely be his last, and dropped down into the abyss.

THIRTY-FIVE

JASON SPLASHED DOWN and kicked headfirst into the black void, the sound of muffled gunshots at his back and flashes of light flickering overhead. The glows from the exploding gunpowder gave him brief glimpses of the underwater cave before him as the bullets broke apart in the water right over his head.

There was only one way out. With his hands extended out in front of him to protect his head, he kicked deeper into the cave, weaving through the narrow, intricate maze that stood between him and his only hope of liberation.

As the sparks subsided at his back, he maneuvered through pure blackness, trying to keep as calm as possible, but soon, the current picked up. The same rushing water that had saved Kidd hundreds of years earlier was pushing against him, trying to shove him back into the cave and right into the hands of the armed criminals.

Jason kicked harder. When the current strengthened even more, he grabbed at the walls and pulled, willing his body closer to the opening, though the opening never came.

His lungs began to throb, then prod, then scream. He tried desperately to keep his heart rate low, but his heart still pounded from the recent chase and the exertion of fighting against the current. Feeling his consciousness fade, Jason knew he likely only had another thirty seconds before blacking out. With no one there to save him, he would inhale a lungful of seawater and drown right there in that cave.

Determined to make it out, Jason dug deep, kicking and navigating and pulling his way out of the cave with every ounce of strength he could muster. Feeling the end drawing near, he raised his hand skyward to feel for a hold. Instead of a rock edge, he felt air and heard a splash. His body desperate, he forced his way up a narrow crack in the top of the cave, his lips just barely breaking free to a pocket of air. He blasted the stale air from his lungs and sucked in two quick, deep lungfuls. The pocket was tiny—barely enough to catch his breath—but it gave him newfound hope.

I can get out of this. I will, or I'll die giving everything I have.

Jason inhaled a final breath and dropped back underwater. He continued his race out of the cave, the current growing even stronger. His lungs began to throb again from the exertion as he pressed on through the blackness and debated heading back to the pocket of air to reevaluate.

Maybe I took a wrong turn. Or maybe I'm going in circles and I'll pop up out of the water with Reznikov's boys.

Just as he was about to turn around, a dim light appeared up ahead. He kicked toward the blurry glow, wondering if his fatigued brain was playing tricks on him. Gripping jutting edges of the tunnel, he shimmied his way around corners, the light giving him newfound vigor. Soon, the cave ended, and he entered a well-lit cavity, and he gazed upon a streak of light pouring out from under a massive growth of table coral.

Jason stared in awe, stunned that he'd escaped the jaws of the menacing cave, but he knew he was far from home free.

This must be the spot Finn tried to fit through.

He grabbed hold of the coral and wedged his way into the space.

It's no use. A child couldn't fit through this.

But Jason had no other option. The jagged limestone bit into his back, slicing his skin and drawing blood. The edges of coral stung his arms and chest, but he only pushed harder. He managed to shimmy his head through, and then a shoulder. With his oxygen exhausted, he began to panic. His lungs were pleading to inhale precious air, and he shook, his eyes spreading wide as he continued to jerk his body harder.

Gritting his teeth, he fought back the intense pain searing from his back, chest, and arms, and muscled his way onward. Jamming himself through the tiny opening, he squeezed his other shoulder through, then grabbed anything he could, finally clawing his ravaged body through the opening and into a cloud of deep red.

On the verge of blacking out, his vision blurred. He'd made it out of the cave but still had to navigate out from under the ledge to reach the surface. His mind went hazy as he kicked and his movements slowed.

He fought with everything he could to stay cognizant, but time had run out. Just as he was about to reach the surface, his body refused to follow his orders, his eyes closed, and everything went dark.

THIRTY-SIX

A **RUSH OF WARMTH** came over Jason's body, and a muffled voice called out his name. He coughed up a mouthful of seawater and blinked like mad. Gasping for air, Jason jerked his head up and wiped his eyes. The sand around him came into focus, as did the lapping surf and a distant ocean.

"Jason, are you all right?" a voice said beside him, the words becoming clear and processed in his foggy mind.

Sherwin Lettsome was kneeling down beside him, a hand placed against his shoulder. "Easy, my friend," the local said. "Slow, calm breaths."

Jason did as instructed, gradually becoming more aware of where he was and the sharp pains nagging at him from all over. He winced as he adjusted his body, feeling the cuts in his back. He sat up and realized the beach surrounding him was empty aside from the islander kneeling beside him.

"You are one lucky gringo," Sherwin said.

Jason pressed his fingers to his temples. "What happened?"

"I was fishing just around the corner there," he said, pointing down the beach. "Heard a commotion. Decided it was best to stay put and not risk drawing attention. Then I look out over the water and see something floating in the current. I realized it was a body. I wouldn't have been able to reach you were it not for this little guy," he said, motioning toward the Seascooter. "You blacked out, Jason. I thought for sure you'd be dead, but the wetsuit kept you afloat. And your head stayed above water." The local shook his head. "You must have a guardian angel looking out for you. You're fortunate to be alive."

Jason ignored the pain and shifted his body around.

"We should stay put," Sherwin added. "Those men are still there. They fired their guns not too long ago."

"They're still there?" Jason said as he forced himself to his feet.

Sherwin jumped up beside him and placed a hand on Jason's arm. "Yes, but you have to stay. You're hurt, my friend."

"It's just a few small scrapes. I have to—"

"There are way too many of them. We should stay here and wait for them to leave."

"Not happening." Jason brushed the sand off and started hustling down the beach.

Sherwin shook his head as he caught up to Jason. "Crazy American."

The two headed down the coast, banking along the edge until they caught a glimpse of the trucks. Creeping beside the mangroves, they witnessed Reznikov and his boys hoisting load after load of treasure chests from the cave a few hundred yards away.

"What now?" Sherwin said. "As I told you before, I'm always armed. But I don't even think *you're* bold enough to take on a dozen fully armed men with nothing but a pistol."

Jason observed the scene, watching carefully as the men piled the chests. Far off to his left, the *Valiant* was still anchored beside the jutting reef. He had more of his team and weapons aboard but no way of contacting them. Plus, the Royal Police patrol boat was still anchored half a mile from the *Valiant*. Jason didn't know what role it was playing, but whoever was aboard clearly wasn't concerned about dealing with Reznikov and his team.

As Jason tried to come up with some form of a plan, leaves crunched and twigs snapped in the foliage to their right. Sherwin snatched the handgun from his waistband and took aim just as Alejandra appeared with her weapon raised.

"It's us, Al," Jason said just as he realized who it was.

Alejandra dashed toward Jason.

"I can't tell you how glad I am to see you," he said, wrapping his arms around her.

"Me, too," she said. "When we saw that explosion at the top of the cave and watched the men swarm inside, we thought you were both goners, for sure." She shook her head in bewilderment. "I tried to draw them away by opening fire after Reznikov entered the cave, but there are too many for me to take on by myself. How in the hell did you manage to get out of there?"

"Long story, but suffice to say, I'll have the scars to prove that squeezing into that underwater cave is possible."

"Jeez," Alejandra said, noticing the tears in the back of his wetsuit.

"I'll be fine," Jason said, waving her off.

He didn't want to think about the injuries he'd sustained. Thinking about them only made them hurt more, and he needed to stay focused on the task at hand.

"Where's Finn?" Jason asked, peering over his shoulder toward the open Caribbean. "He aboard the *Valiant*? We need to get ahold of him."

"He's over here," Alejandra said gravely. She led them into the brush, and Jason laid eyes on their Venezuelan friend, resting on his back against a small rise. He was dazed and had a branch tied around his right leg. He tried to move when he saw them approach but winced.

"Easy," Alejandra said.

Jason knelt beside his friend. "What happened?"

"Reznikov's men opened fire as we approached on the RHIB," Finn said. "We were just about to fly out of their view around the point when they blew the port pontoon, and we flipped. My leg was smashed between the engine and the reef, and it cracked." He looked past Jason and Sherwin. "Where's Charlotte?"

Jason paused a moment, then looked in the direction of the commotion from the heavy machinery and criminals.

"They took her?" Alejandra said.

Jason sighed. "More like she rejoined them."

Finn adjusted his leg splint. "What?"

"It doesn't matter," Jason said. "She's not on our side. Never was, apparently. But we can't think about that." He stood and thought for a moment. "We got our butts kicked in the first round, but the fight's not over yet. Any word from Scottie?"

"He's on the police boat," Alejandra said. "Apparently, Reznikov has some friends in high places."

"Well, they won't be able to stop us. Once we take Reznikov down, they'll fall. We're gonna blow the lid on this whole thing."

The group fell silent, and Finn looked around at their battered, weary bodies. "How exactly are we supposed to do that?"

Jason thought again. They had the element of surprise on their side. Reznikov no doubt thought he was dead, and the Russian most likely believed Alejandra and Finn were also down. They could use that to their advantage, but like Sherwin said minutes earlier, how could they take down so many armed thugs when they were still vastly outnumbered and outgunned?

Just as Jason opened his mouth, a low hum echoed across the tropical sky.

"What's that?" Finn said, raising his eyebrows.

The group squinted into the bright blue above, searching for the source of the sound. Sherwin was the first to spot it, shielding his eyes from the sun.

"We've got a plane incoming," he said, climbing up onto a stump. "And a monster one at that."

Jason watched as the plane soared into view on the horizon. The group marveled at its size as the craft came around, flying straight toward the island.

"Monster is right," Jason said. "That thing's enormous. How big is the runway on Anegada?"

"August George Airport has a tarmac of about half a mile," Sherwin said.

Jason folded his arms. "That's way too short for a plane like that to take off."

Alejandra said, "I don't think it's using the runway."

The colossal aircraft descended steadily, creeping toward the calm blue just beyond the reef. The pilot brought down the fuselage of the seaplane onto the water, splashing down smoothly and easing back on the throttles. They watched as the enormous craft turned toward the shore, its propellers pushing it through an opening in the reef. The plane turned around slowly when it reached the shore, then the back opened up, and a massive door landed on the beach just up from the surf beside the three trucks.

"Whatever we do, it better be quick," Sherwin said, "because whoever those guys are, they're about to make off with all those chests."

THIRTY-SEVEN

NIKOLAI REZNIKOV WATCHED as his quarry vanished behind a veil of pungent smoke pluming from the barrel of his Makarov. The sound of exploding gunpowder boomed in the tight confines of the cave. He gripped his weapon tight and narrowed his gaze, hoping to catch a glimpse of Jason Wake's dead body. But as the gunshot subsided, he saw no sign of the American and heard only the shuffling of feet as Jason took off deeper into the cave.

"Go get him!" Reznikov barked, aiming his pistol into the blackness. "I want his body filled with bullets . . . on sight!"

Two of his men stormed past, shining their flashlights and aiming their weapons as they hustled into the narrow opening.

"You can't run, Wake!" Reznikov added, his face contorting with anger. "There's nowhere to go."

He'd wanted to finish Wake off himself—to watch as the cocky young man collapsed into painful anguish. To stare him in the eyes as the life drained from him.

The punk had been a sharp thorn deep in his side for long enough, and he wanted to show the man what happened to people who crossed him. His face formed a smile, and he lowered his weapon as the glow from his men's flashlights disappeared as they chased after Wake. He relished the idea of the guy having to run for it, to struggle for his life in the dark, only to meet the same fate—to feel the fear and the helplessness take hold.

Reznikov turned as the machine high above him groaned, lowering the metal platform back into the cave. Charlotte had been put into one of the trucks. Three more men arrived on the platform, their weapons raised.

"Go after Wake," Reznikov ordered, stabbing a finger at one of the soldiers.

The subordinate nodded, clicked on his flashlight, and took off into the cave.

Just a little insurance to make sure Wake's finished off for good, Reznikov thought.

Sliding his forty-five into a worn leather holster, Reznikov ordered the rest of his men to continue loading up the treasure. The group carried chest after chest onto the platform and lifted two stacks full up onto the beach before the three men returned.

Reznikov turned as they appeared from the darkness. "Where's the body?" he snarled, scrutinizing the three men. "I heard the gunshots. You killed him, then?"

The men fell silent.

Finally, the middle guy strode forward. "We left it back there," he said, pointing into the cave. "His body's filled with holes, and he's lying facedown in a pool of water."

Reznikov grinned, then turned toward the others. "Good. Now, help them load up the rest of the treasure. We have a schedule to keep."

Reznikov climbed aboard the platform for its next trip up, hopping out onto the sand when it reached the top and feeling the heat of the tropical sun. Beside the trucks were piles of old wooden chests stacked five feet high and thirty wide—a mountain of pirate treasure.

Reznikov shielded his eyes from the sun and scanned the beach. Six of his men were standing by at the perimeter of the hole, rifles at the ready, and two more were beside the trucks and operating the winch, while the rest were hauling up the treasure.

The going was slow, but they kept at it. After half an hour of carrying and loading and raising and stacking, they'd removed almost every chest from the cave.

Reznikov checked the time. Moments after he did, he heard an engine on the horizon and smiled as he laid eyes on a distant aircraft soaring toward the island.

One of the men witnessed Reznikov's reaction to the plane. "What's going on, boss? I thought we were transporting these out on the ferry."

"Just a little change in plans," Reznikov snickered, "to ensure that we receive the full cut. I always take care of my own. Besides, after the losses we've suffered, we deserve a bigger slice of the pie."

The plane banked around, then splashed down just beyond the reef. As it motored through an opening in the shallows, heading toward their position, Reznikov's phone buzzed to life.

"What is this, Nikolai?" a man with an English accent said as he answered. "The plan was to load the trucks onto the ferry at Setting Point."

"Plans change, Calvert. The ferry has been compromised."

"I've received no such word."

"I've been doing this since before you were born. You will heed to my wisdom."

"I swear, Nikolai, if you cross me, I'll—"

"I wouldn't think of it, Calvert. The transfer of funds and the acquisition will still unfold as planned."

The governor sighed. "You'd better—"

Reznikov hung up as the rear door of the seaplane opened and a metal platform extended out onto the beach.

"We're still transferring the governor a percentage?" a man beside Reznikov said.

"That fool will get what he deserves—absolutely nothing. This treasure's ours, and I'll be damned if I share it with some politician. I already have a buyer ready."

Two guys operated a cart with rubber tires down the ramp from the aircraft and onto the sand, then they shot Reznikov a thumbs-up.

The Russian smiled and turned to his men. "Load up. It's time to get the hell off this island."

THIRTY-EIGHT

WATCHING AS REZNIKOV'S men began carting Kidd's treasure onto the plane, Jason clenched a fist. He veered off from the group, looking out over Budrock Pond to his right, then set his sights on the beach at their backs. There, still resting on the sand, was the Seascooter Sherwin had used to save his life.

Jason wiped the sweat from his brow, then rubbed his chin as he watched the plane being loaded. "Sherwin," he said, striding back to the others and pointing at the Seascooter. "That thing have any juice left?"

"'Bout half a charge, I'd say."

He paused again, then peered down the shoreline of the pond.

"What's going on, Jase?" Alejandra said. "What are you thinking?"

He focused toward the deeper water of the lake but couldn't see the small grassy area on the shore where they'd entered from.

"My gear bag still over there?" Jason said.

Finn shrugged. "Should be, unless Reznikov's thugs moved it."

Jason nodded. "All right. You guys stay here and keep hidden. I'll be right back."

Keeping low, he crept through the brush, then slid down a muddy bank to the shore of the pond.

"Where are you going?" Alejandra asked.

"To get my scuba gear."

"You mean the gear that's in the cave that Reznikov and his goons are currently looting?"

Jason didn't have time to answer or explain his plan. He needed to get moving. If his stuff on the shore had been moved, or if his scuba gear down in the cave had been tampered with, they'd have to scrap his dicey idea and come up with a new plan . . . quickly.

As stealthily as he could, Jason shuffled down the backside of the mangroves, his feet sinking into the mud with every other step. When he neared the small grassy clearing, he peeked up just enough to see that his gear bag was still there. Less than a hundred yards beyond it were the trucks and the commotion, and the armed men were keeping watch around them.

It was now or never.

Calming his breathing, Jason dashed for the clearing, then dropped onto his chest beside the gear bag. Unzipping the main compartment, he pulled out a spare dive mask, then army-crawled back down to the pond. Wading into the water, he slid in until it was nearly over his head.

Let's try not to black out this time, he thought as he inhaled a deep breath and submerged.

He moved quickly to the bottom, swam through the opening in the brick wall, then navigated his way through the cave. Having already traveled the same path just over an hour earlier, it was fresh in his mind, and he reached the surface in the first underground chamber with oxygen to spare.

He slowly broke free, listening carefully and keeping his eyes peeled for any movement. There was no sign of activity that deep into the cave, but he could hear voices from the treasure cavern.

He climbed out of the water and headed straight for the two BCDs and tanks and fins that he and Charlotte had left. Grabbing his gear, Jason reentered the water, then traversed the distance back into the pond,

265

managing to haul the gear back to the others without being spotted.

Gassed, he collapsed onto a knee and caught his breath.

"Great," Finn said, eyeing the gear. "Now we're saved."

Jason panted. "Hey, I figured you guys would have a little more faith in me after all we've been through."

"We do," Alejandra said, "but they're wrapping up." She stuck a thumb toward Reznikov and his boys. "So, whatever's going on inside that head of yours, you might want to let us in on it."

Jason told them his plan as quickly and articulately as he could. He'd don the gear and use the Seascooter to reach the plane without being spotted. Then, once he was ready to board it, the three of them would attack the criminals from the shoreline, covering Jason as he entered the plane.

Alejandra bit her lip. "Even if you do make it onto that thing without being spotted, you won't exactly be home free."

"Al's right," Finn said. "Just you against everyone on that aircraft?"

"I'm banking on you three drawing most of the group away from the plane. And I don't need to take everyone out . . . just Reznikov. He's the mastermind behind this whole thing. We take him out, the others will fall."

"Maybe. . . ." Sherwin said, thinking it over. "But if you kill this guy Reznikov, his remaining men will kill you."

Jason shrugged. "So be it. At least Reznikov won't get away with this. At least the people of Anegada will still have their home."

Sherwin shook his head. "I'm not sure you're thinking this through enough."

"Regardless," Finn said, "even if you do reach the plane, how are we gonna know when you're there?"

Jason glanced at his watch and realized that it was almost eleven-thirty. "Thirty-five after. That's when you guys make your move."

"That gives you five minutes," Alejandra said.

He shouldered the BCD and snatched the fins. "Then I guess I'd better get moving. And Sherwin, thank you for everything. You've done more than enough. Please don't feel like you have to—"

He waved Jason off. "This is my home, and I will protect it with you."

Jason placed a hand on the man's shoulder, then shot Alejandra and Finn a reassuring look before bolting down the beach. He snatched the Seascooter mid-stride, then splashed into the surf. Once waist deep, he donned his dive gear, slid his mask over his face, then dropped down into the Caribbean. Leveling his body, he finned out until he was in ten feet of water, then powered on the Seascooter and held on tight.

The propeller accelerated, churning up bubbles and dragging him through the colorful landscape. Keeping his eyes locked forward, he navigated around shallow reefs, rocketing at over seven knots through cuts and closing the distance between him and the plane as fast as he could. Seeing the massive hull up ahead near the shore, he checked the time and saw that he had all of thirty seconds before the others were going to make their move.

Talk about cutting it close, he thought, giving the Seascooter everything it had and flying toward the plane.

He reached the aircraft with just seconds to spare. Letting go of the machine, he finned toward the back of the plane, unclipped his BCD, and slid out of his fins when he could stand. Gripping the pistol, he raised it shoulder height and broke free of the water right alongside the ramp. Jason was greeted by the sound of roaring propellers, the plane's engines starting, and the men loading up the final chests.

He scanned the scene for Reznikov, but he wasn't there. Clusters of his men were climbing into trucks, and two of them were hauling up the last load of chests as others moved in from the perimeter.

Jason surfaced for just four seconds when gunfire erupted.

THIRTY-NINE

THE SCENE AWOKE like a spooked hornet's nest as one of Reznikov's thugs took a round to the chest, falling backward onto the beach. Bullets rained down on the group, and a second guy was hit before they took cover, raised their weapons, and returned fire, sending streams of automatic gunfire into the brush beside them.

Jason heard Reznikov yell out from inside the plane, ordering the two men to continue loading the final cart of chests into the aircraft. Doing as they were told, the men leaned forward and put their backs into it, shoving the big cart up the ramp and into the plane. After pushing it all the way up, the men stormed back toward the beach and opened fire.

Jason watched carefully, waiting for the right time to strike.

Another criminal went down, struck in the side and bloodied as he fell onto the sand. Three of the men took cover behind the trucks, shooting their weapons chaotically into the mangroves.

"Get your asses back in here!" Reznikov shouted from inside. "We're taking off!"

The Russian's voice died off as the sounds of the engines and propellers got louder. The massive aircraft lurched, then accelerated away from the beach, and the two men hustled backward toward the cargo bay. As the trailing guy spun around, his eyes bulged as he saw Jason in the water right below him.

It took the man a split second to react to what he was seeing, and Jason used the moment of confusion to his advantage. Springing out of the shallows, he grabbed a fistful of the guy's shirt with his left hand, then yanked him off the ramp and into the water. As the guy struggled to retaliate, Jason relieved the thug of his pistol and pressed the barrel into the guy's gut, muffling the blast as he pulled the trigger and buried a 9mm round in his abdomen. The guy went lifeless, and just as Jason turned around, the second criminal ran down the ramp.

Jason raised his newly acquired weapon and pulled the trigger, putting a round through the guy's left kneecap. His momentum still at full speed, the aggressor tumbled, falling over the ramp and crashing right into Jason, who tried his best to go with the fall, twisting as the guy's big frame slammed into him. The man was a good fighter, but his injured leg gave Jason the upper hand as he manhandled the criminal beneath the waves, then bashed his skull with the grip of his pistol.

Jason burst back out of the water and gasped, catching his breath as the plane continued to accelerate away from him. With no choice but to go after the aircraft, and with the remaining criminals on the beach aware of his presence, Jason bolted into a sprint, splashing toward the ramp. As he targeted the metal walkway and pumped his arms, he watched it rise from the water.

Needing to dive to make it, Jason hurled his body through the air and reached as high and far as he could, his fingers gripping the edge of the ramp and his body swinging forward. As bullets splashed into the water behind him, Jason muscled himself over the edge of the metal and barely slipped through before it slammed shut.

He tumbled down into the plane, bullets peppering the metal at his back and sending sparks before it closed. Sliding down the inside of the ramp, he rolled and caught himself against a stack of strapped-down treasure chests.

FORTY

ALEJANDRA PEEKED AT her watch, then crawled closer to the trucks. Reznikov's men patrolled the area as the final cart of chests were rolled up into the plane. She scanned the water beside the massive aircraft, but saw no sign of Jason.

All right, where are you, Jase?

She stared at her timepiece, monitoring the ticking second hand. He had thirty seconds to get into position before they opened fire on the criminals.

Alejandra lowered her body even more as a guy looked her way. Keeping herself pressed to the sand, she contorted along a thick tangle of branches, just thirty yards from the men. Her heart beating hard, she knew if they realized she was there before the moment of attack came, she'd be a goner.

When the criminal turned away from her and helped with the winch, she peeked across the beach to the other side of the hole where Finn and Sherwin were hiding out at the edge of the mangroves. The seconds ticked down, and just as they were about to hit the designated time, Alejandra spotted movement in the water beside the top of the plane ramp. When the dark silhouette of a diver appeared in the shadows, she gripped her pistol.

Here we go.

Gunshots filled the air as Finn opened fire first. One of the criminals went down right away, and the others scrambled, fighting for cover and yelling out as they tried to figure out where their attackers were. More shots filled the air, this time coming from the opposite side of Alejandra as Sherwin engaged, taking down another one of the criminals.

As the men took cover and opened fire, sending sporadic sprays of bullets through the foliage, Alejandra rose and moved in. She sprang toward the closest thug who was kneeling behind the front of one of the trucks. The moment he realized Alejandra was there, the Latina grabbed him from behind, kicked a heel into the back of his left knee, then struck him across the temple, knocking him out.

As the man's body fell to the sand, a second criminal spotted the act and opened fire, sending a storm of bullets sparking against the frame of the truck. Alejandra dropped to her chest and crawled around the unconscious guy, taking aim in the space under the truck and firing off two rounds. One struck her attacker's foot. His lower body swung out from under him and his face smacked against the beach. A second shot to the chest finished him off.

Crawling to the back of the truck and rising to a knee, Alejandra watched as Jason sprinted through the water, splashing as he chased after the plane accelerating away from the shore. Reznikov's two remaining thugs opened fire on Jase, pelting rounds against the rising ramp as he gripped the edge and flung his body up and into the aircraft just before the metal slammed shut.

With the two men's attention diverted, Alejandra closed in. She put a round into the back of the first guy, and he grunted and shot bullets skyward as he lurched to the sand. The second guy spun quickly, dropping to a knee and aiming his rifle at Alejandra. She dove, colliding with the guy's shins and swiping his lower half out from under him before tackling him to the sand. The two rolled and struggled, knocking each other's weapons free.

With the sounds of the plane roaring at their backs, the two exchanged blows and fought for the upper hand as they came to a stop beside the edge of the blown-out hole into the cave. The guy was bigger and stronger, but Alejandra used her skills to her advantage, along with her lack of an instinct to fight fair. As the guy geared up to pound a meaty fist into her face, Alejandra kneed him in the groin, and his body shook and fell sideways.

Forcing him off her, Alejandra spun as the guy yelled out and forced himself to his feet. He snatched a knife from his hip, but before he could move in for a strike, Alejandra planted her left leg and bashed her right heel into his chest. The man jolted backward from the blow, his body flying over the edge of the cliff. From her vantage point, all Alejandra could see was his contorted body as he disappeared over the edge. Their final adversary let out a shrill cry before hitting the bottom of the cave with a loud, bone-cracking thud.

Alejandra grabbed her pistol from the sand, and after ensuring that the scene was clear of enemies, crept to the edge and caught sight of the man's motionless body sprawled out over rocks at the bottom of the cave below.

Alejandra strode to the surf and watched as the roaring aircraft continued to accelerate out through a cut in the reef, then lifted up from the water.

Finn and Sherwin appeared from the brush at her back, their weapons raised as they combed the area.

Still tracking the aircraft as it soared into the sky, Alejandra whispered, "Godspeed, Jase."

FORTY-ONE

SCOTT AWOKE TO a loud humming noise reverberating through the hull of the patrol boat. He sat on the cold floor of a small holding area, his hands cuffed to a steel eyebolt in the bulkhead at his back. The space was so small and cramped with piping he could barely see the door ten feet away.

Adjusting his position, he craned his neck to view the only source of light in the space: a tiny porthole. As the humming noises grew louder and the boat began to vibrate, Scott realized they were the sounds of engines and rotors and that they were coming in from the west. Peering toward the glass, he caught a brief glimpse of a low-flying seaplane, its hulking frame blocking out the sun for a moment before roaring past and heading toward Anegada.

A plane? Reznikov's going to swipe this thing right out from under them.

Since the cuffs had been fastened too tight for Scott to force his hands free, he had to consider alternate methods of escape. Reaching around the back of his dive watch, he felt for a tiny multi-tool kit he'd installed for emergencies but sighed when he realized it wasn't there.

Of course they found and removed it.

A valve cap with a metal locking device was to his right, and the mechanism contained a zinc-plated cotter pin that appeared just thin enough to fit into the small keyhole of the handcuffs.

He slid the chain of his shackles as far as he could until his left hand touched the eye bolt, then reached for the locking device. Still inches shy, he angled his shoulders back and stretched his right foot as far as it could go, just grazing the bottom of the cotter pin. As smoothly as he could, Scott pressed the rubber sole against the pin, sliding the metal device up out of the aperture, then stopped and relaxed just before it reached the top. He only had one chance to push it free, and if he got it wrong, the pin could tumble out of reach.

Scott held his breath as he carefully dislodged the fastener. As the small piece of metal fell, he arched his shoe back, and the pin bounced down the vamp before clinking to the hard floor beside him.

He let out a relieved sigh, then kicked the clasp toward his hands with his heel. Gripping the pin, he tried to bend it into an L shape, but the metal was too strong. Just as he was about to say "screw it" and shove the fastener into the keyhole, hoping it would do the trick, his eyes rested on the insulated piping to his right. He peeled off a small piece of foam, then pressed the pin against the hot piping. After holding it there for thirty seconds, he brought the clasp away and bent the warmed, more-malleable metal to form his desired shape.

Having been trained in tactical prisoner scenarios for years, Scott slid his newly formed tool into the keyhole and jimmied the lock until the latches released. A smile came to his face as the ratchet teeth slipped free, allowing him to pull out his left hand.

Scott rubbed his liberated wrist for a moment before attacking the second cuff. The sounds of the nearby plane engines and rotors had quieted, and he guessed it wouldn't take long for the Russian criminal and his men to load up the treasure and make a mad break back into the sky.

While jimmying the second cuff, approaching foot-steps sounded from just outside the door. With no time to beat the lock, he rushed to his feet and cut across the room, slipping behind the door just before it creaked open.

A short, young police officer stepped inside, then froze. "What the he—"

Scott pounced, wrapping his left arm around the guy's neck while covering his mouth with the right, then yanked the squirming, groaning officer back into the shadows. The young man didn't stand a chance, and his body quickly went limp in Scott's arms.

With the door still open, Scott listened carefully. When he didn't hear any backup, he grabbed the deformed cotter pin and finished what he'd started, removing the second cuff. Kneeling, Scott flipped over the unconscious officer and slid a Browning 9mm pistol from the man's hip. He concealed the pistol in his waistband, wanting to use it only as a last resort.

He poked his head out the door, and seeing nobody, crept down the short walkway and up a narrow set of stairs to a custom lounge. The cabin cruiser was sleek and functional, having been retrofitted to suit the needs of the police force. A long metal desk with laptops ran along the port bulkhead, and a heavy-duty table was bolted down in the middle, flanked by padded bench seats.

Voices emanated from the flybridge directly over his head, and with the interior pilot's station empty, he knew the rest of the officers had to be topside. Peeking out the windscreen, he saw Governor David Calvert still up on the bow and talking animatedly into his cellphone.

Scott crept through the aft door and into the warm afternoon air, then he dropped down, taking cover along the outer bulkhead. Edging along the starboard side of the vessel, he caught a glimpse of officers up in the bridge as he closed in on the governor.

"The plan was to load the trucks onto the ferry at Setting Point," Scott heard Calvert frantically say into his phone. "I've received no such word."

While Calvert was occupied, Scott crept closer, wanting to catch him off guard.

The politician made a fist. "I swear, Nikolai, if you cross me, I'll—" He cleared his throat. "You'd better. If you don't, I don't care if . . . Hello? Nikolai?" The governor jerked the phone in front of his face and stared at the screen. "Dammit."

Calvert stomped against the starboard bow and stared out toward the beach while Reznikov's men loaded stacks of chests into the back of the aircraft.

Scott withdrew the Browning pistol and stood tall. "Still trusting Reznikov?" he said, aiming his weapon. "You're even dumber than I thought."

The governor spun around, spooked by Scott's words and nearly stumbling as they locked eyes on each other.

"Mr. Cooper," he said, his eyes filling with anger.

Scott stomped toward Calvert, keeping his sight leveled on the man's tie. "You said you read about me. Clearly, you didn't read enough." He gripped a fistful of Calvert's shirt and hovered the barrel of his handgun over the man's pale face.

"What . . . what do you want?"

"Stop the plane from taking off," Scott said.

"It's too late," Calvert rasped. "There's nothing that can be done."

A door suddenly slammed open at Scott's back. He spun around, using the corrupt politician as a human shield as Sergeant Graham and two other officers stormed onto the main deck with their weapons raised.

"Freeze, Mr. Cooper!" Graham yelled.

"Shoot him!" Calvert squealed before Scott tightened his grip.

Graham strode closer. "Let go of the governor."

"Not another step," Scott said. "Like I said, you're on the wrong side here." Keeping Calvert in place, he slipped out the governor's phone. "Here," Scott said, tossing the device to the sergeant. "Your governor's been communicating with Nikolai Reznikov, a Russian criminal, who at this moment, is about to make off with hundreds of millions in lost gold. As I said, my name is Scott Cooper. I'm a former commander in the US Navy and a former senator. My team and I are here to stop the Russian criminal and this corrupt politician who's been backing him up."

"He's lying!" Calvert spat. "Shoot him. Shoot him, now!"

Graham froze, looking back and forth between the two before homing in on the cellphone.

"I'm not your enemy," Scott said. "Look at the call history and messages. He's been playing you and working with the criminals all along."

The sergeant ordered his men to keep their weapons aimed at Scott, then stepped aside and thumbed through the messages on the phone.

After a minute of scanning, the officer sighed, then pocketed the device. "I have my orders, Mr. Cooper. I can't just break them. As a former naval officer, you know that as well as I do."

Scott shook his head. "We won't get a second chance at this."

The moment the words left Scott's lips, the sounds of loud, popping gunfire echoed across the water.

"Get down!" Graham yelled, hitting the deck.

Scott remained on his feet but turned around, focusing his attention on the far-off shoreline. He watched as Reznikov's men scattered, taking cover as they were engaged from all sides. The Russians retaliated, firing off rounds into the nearby brush.

Scott's eyes widened as the seaplane began to accelerate away from the beach. "Clock's ticking. What's it gonna be, Graham?"

The sergeant swallowed hard, then stared at the thundering aircraft. Taking in a deep breath, he shook his head and gestured at the two men at his flanks. "Lower your weapons."

The two men did as they were ordered, and Graham turned back toward Scott and Calvert.

Scott gave a slight nod as the tension of the heated standoff abated, but he needed no reminder that the battle was far from over. "Now we need to stop that plane."

Graham stepped higher onto the bow for a better view of the aircraft, then reached for his radio.

"What is this?" Calvert shrieked, his nostrils flaring. "What the hell are you idiots doing? Kill him, now!"

Sergeant Graham and his fellow officers ignored the command and radioed the officers on the nearby interceptor. The sergeant knew their cabin cruiser was too slow to reach the accelerating aircraft but hoped that the speed demon patrol boat could live up to its name.

Just as Graham opened his mouth to give the order, Calvert went berserk. He elbowed Scott in the gut, then lunged toward Graham. Before he'd made it a full step, Scott pounced on him from behind, grabbing him by his jacket, whacking him in his right ear, then manhandling his fragile frame into the starboard bow. Calvert cried as he hit the deck, his hands pressed to his bleeding forehead.

Graham lowered his radio in preparation for the failed attack, then scowled at the governor. "I never liked him anyway."

Scott watched as the plane picked up more speed, its hull slicing through an opening in the reef. He'd convinced the crew he was on their side, but it was just moments too late. Before an order could be given to attempt to block the plane's escape, the aircraft lifted up from the water, soaring into the open blue sky.

FORTY-TWO

JASON JOSTLED TO a stop at the base of the pile of treasure chests. His mind in a daze, he collected himself and caught his breath, then realized his pistol was gone. He'd lost it during his mad dash to chase down the plane and climb into the back before being squashed by the ramp.

When he peeked around the wooden chests, he spotted Reznikov standing near the forward bulkhead. He had his pistol aimed toward Jason, and Charlotte stood stoically at his side.

"It's over, Mr. Wake," Reznikov snarled. "Look around you. In eight hours, I will melt down this gold and sell it for a fortune. As I have told you, I always win. One way or another. Despite all of your efforts, you have failed." The wretch glanced at Charlotte, standing rigid as stone, then back at Jason. "I must say . . . As much as I will enjoy reaping the financial rewards of this conquest, the look on your face when you realized that Miss Murchison has been working for me the entire time is an image I shall savor forever. Did you really believe I could be taken down so easily? I've been traveling the world over and have defeated men like you since long before you were born, and I will continue doing so long after you're dead. How did you think we found you in Scotland?" The Russian smirked. "Yes, Mr. Wake, she has been playing you the entire time. And now you will suffer the painful consequences of your naïve actions." The Russian took aim, pointing the barrel of his Makarov pistol at Jason's chest. "Goodbye, Mr. Wake."

As the words left his lips, a hand swept across the Russian's mid-section. Charlotte had lunged at Reznikov, forcing his gun hand skyward. He pulled the trigger, the explosion deafening in the closed-in space. The round shot through the air and burst a gash through the top of the fuselage, giving a tiny glimpse to the bright outside.

After redirecting Reznikov's aim, Charlotte tried to relieve the man of his weapon, but the Russian was strong and hard and no stranger to physical conflict. He let out a low growl and punched Charlotte in the shoulder. The petite woman fell to her hands and knees, and when she looked back up, Reznikov smacked her across the face with his Makarov. She shrieked and then fell motionless to the floor.

"You're a foolish woman!" Reznikov spat.

"Not as foolish as you!" Jason fired back.

Using the brief scuffle to dart across the cargo bay, Jason gripped Reznikov's gun hand and finished what Charlotte had started, thrusting the killer sideways and slamming the weapon into the stacks of treasure chests beside them. The gun fell free, tumbling to the deck and coming to rest on the opposite side of the space.

Squeezing his right hand into a right fist, Jason bashed his knuckles into Reznikov's cheek, then ripped the polished cane from his hand and swung it into the Russian's side. He collected himself against the forward bulkhead, his upper body hunched over as the aircraft continued picking up speed.

Jason was forced to crouch down as the plane shook and its nose tilted up. The craft lifted off the water, roaring and accelerating high into the air.

Wiping the blood dripping down the side of his pale, weathered face, Reznikov spat into the corner, then gave Jason a death stare. "You still have no idea who you're messing with, boy." The Russian criminal slid a black, twelve-inch steel blade from his belt, the sharpened metal glistening under the dim overhead lights. He pointed the tip at Jason, then lowered into a fighting stance. "Your move, Wake."

Jason didn't wait for a second invitation. Still gripping the ivory cane, he lunged toward Reznikov and swung it toward the man's waist. Fast for his age, and with a lifetime of experience in deadly situations, the Russian avoided the attack and stabbed his blade. The countermove drove Jason to shift into an unbalanced position, and Reznikov capitalized on it, shouldering Jason backward and nearly knocking him to the deck.

Reznikov followed up the strike with a flurry of swipes and stabs, backing Jason up against the stack of chests. "This blade has taken down lions in the African plains and jaguars in the Amazon."

Fatigued from the dozen injuries he'd suffered that day, Jason caught Reznikov's wrist and pressed with all his strength. The Russian's blade was just inches from Jason's flesh.

"And you're the next victim!" Reznikov yanked his hand free and stabbed the knife toward Jason's face.

Jason jerked sideways at the last second, the tip of the blade grazing the fringes of his hair before piercing deep into one of the wooden chests. As Reznikov struggled to dislodge his burrowed weapon, Jason landed a hard punch to his jaw. Dazed, Reznikov stepped backward, giving Jason just enough space between them to rear back the cane and bash it into Reznikov's chest. The Russian collapsed, wheezing at Jason's feet as he tried to fight back the pain.

"It's you who has lost," Jason said.

He forced the blade free from the chest, tossed the cane, then stepped toward Reznikov. Reaching to grip a fistful of the struggling criminal's shirt, Jason froze as the deck shuddered beneath his feet. The plane angled sharply, turning to the right.

As the deck continued to tilt, Jason reached back and clutched the rope securing the tower of treasure chests. With nothing to grab onto, Reznikov's body tumbled backward, rolling twice before slamming into the opposite side of the fuselage. He coughed and wheezed, trying to catch his breath, and when he peered up toward Jason, his eyes rested on his pistol lying on the floor beside him.

Jason gasped as the Russian gripped his weapon, then sneered. "It seems, Mr. Wake, that fortune favors me."

Needing to make a move, but with Reznikov too far away to take him down before he opened fire, Jason slashed the nylon rope with the razor-sharp blade. The snapping fibers freed the mountain of chests, and the mass of heavy objects toppled over in an avalanche across the bay. Reznikov froze in terror, then let out an ear-splitting shriek as the chests rumbled violently, smashing into him and crushing his body.

FORTY-THREE

JASON HELD TIGHT to what remained of the rope and watched as Nikolai Reznikov met his end. All he could see was the criminal's hand releasing the pistol and letting it rattle to the deck. The rest of his body was completely buried by Kidd's treasure—the very treasure Reznikov had been so desperate to find and claim for himself.

As the plane stabilized, the pile tumbled and spread across the middle of the hold. Jason let go when he noticed Charlotte lying in the right corner of the bulkhead, her lifeless body having slid across the floor during the plane's turn. Battered from the scuffle, he staggered across the space, dropped down beside her, and placed her head on his thigh. Brushing aside her short dark hair, he looked into her eyes as they blinked open.

She let out a breath, fighting to remain conscious. "I'm sorry, Jason," she said, panting for air.

The side of her face was bleeding from Reznikov striking her down. "They have my father . . . Nikolai said he'd kill him if I didn't—"

"It's all right," Jason said, holding her close. "He's gone now. And you're going to be okay."

Suddenly, the plane jostled again, this time tilting forward as the engines whined. Clasping the edge of a tie-down rail, Jason looked up as he heard a commotion coming from the other side of the bulkhead. Knowing he still had at least the two pilots and perhaps even more of Reznikov's thugs to deal with, he repositioned Charlotte, then jumped to his feet with Reznikov's knife still clutched in his right hand.

He reached the door just as it burst open, where the lanky pilot scrutinized Jason quizzically, then focused on Reznikov's mangled body across the bay.

"Easy," Jason said, holding up the knife.

The pilot snarled and pounced toward Jason, throwing a wide right hook. Leaning back, Jason struck him with a fierce sidekick, mashing his heel into the guy's chest and sending him flying back into the cockpit.

Before the pilot could recover, Jason closed the distance and put the guy in a rear choke hold right behind the pilot's seat. A younger man in the co-pilot's seat unclipped his harness, his face frozen in shock.

"You're going to turn around and land this thing back near Anegada," Jason said, eyeing both men. "Understand?"

The senior aviator squirmed in Jason's grasp. "Go to hell!"

The angered pilot whirled around, jutting a hidden blade toward Jason's neck, but Jason spun him into the left side of the flight deck, ramming his skull against the metal.

As the pilots' body slumped to the floor, Jason turned his attention to the co-pilot. The young man made a last-ditch effort to take Jason down by reaching to his left for a stowed handgun. Jason lunged toward his assailant, taking him down by knocking the butt of Reznikov's knife into the side of his head. Unconscious, the co-pilot fell forward, his body draping over the control column.

The aircraft lurched forward, and Jason was barely able to catch himself against the back of the seat. Charlotte screamed as the plane angled, sliding into the cockpit. Jason barely managed to catch her and keep her stable before reaching forward and gripping the yoke with both hands.

"Strap in!" Jason yelled, helping Charlotte into the co-pilot's seat.

A quick sweep of the instrument panel told him that they were rapidly losing altitude.

"Can you fly a plane like this?" she gasped. "Because that ocean's getting very close."

"First time for everything," Jason said, muscling the unconscious co-pilot aside, strapping in, and grabbing hold of the yoke.

Though he'd been flying for years and had recently completed his seaplane rating qualifications, his experience was with much smaller aircraft. Gripping the control column tight, he looked over the controls and checked the gauges. He eased back on the throttle, then pulled back on the yoke, causing the massive aircraft to shake and arch skyward.

"We're coming in too steep!" he said, trying his best to keep control and lift them out of the freefall.

They jolted forward as he reversed the throttle and struggled to control the craft. But the plane was too big and laden, and it had already picked up too much downward momentum.

"Hold on!" he yelled as the blue Caribbean magnified in the windshield.

Still pulling back as hard as he could on the yoke, he extended all of the flaps to increase drag, then dipped the nose up and leveled the aircraft just as the hull struck the water. Jason and Charlotte jarred forward, slamming into the nylon harnesses as the hull cut into the sea.

Jason held on tight, letting out a triumphant sigh as the plane gradually slowed. He thought for sure that given their speed, the aircraft would break apart on impact, but the frame held together, quaking like mad as it slowed to a violent stop. The massive wake formed from the landing splashed over the plane, nearly covering the windshield as it lifted them up and rolled ahead.

In the quiet following the utter chaos, all Jason could hear was his heart thumping in his chest. He unclipped his harness, then practically fell out of his seat as the fatigue and pains bore down on him.

Charlotte's eyes were bigger than the sea in front of them. "This was all my fault," she said. "I never should have—"

Jason pressed a finger to her lips. "It's over now."

The craft floated lifelessly in the middle of the sea. Reznikov was dead. His men had all been dealt with. Kidd's treasure was secure, and the people of Anegada no longer had to worry about losing their home.

"It's over."

FORTY-FOUR

CHARLOTTE NOTICED JASON'S wounds for the first time. "Jeez," she said as she examined the cuts through his wetsuit and the bruises on his face. "How are you still breathing?"

Jason winced. "Now that the adrenaline's wearing off, I'm sure I'll start to feel it more . . . especially my back."

He leaned forward, and Charlotte placed a hand to her mouth when she saw the cuts through the shredded neoprene. She found a first aid kit in a locker and cracked it open. As she went to work on his wounds, Jason grabbed the cockpit radio only to find that it wasn't working.

"Of course," he said.

Charlotte scanned the water surrounding them. "At least we won't be hard to find."

"Provided this thing wasn't damaged," Jason said, inspecting the metal frame of the aircraft. "You hear flowing water, let me know."

Charlotte grabbed a handful of gauze pad pouches and a tube of antibacterial cream and went to work on Jason's wounds.

Ten minutes after the aircraft splashed down, a boat came into view.

"You mind handing me those binos from the locker?" Jason said.

Between applying antiseptic and gauze, Charlotte grabbed them and handed them over.

Jason focused through the lenses and clenched his jaw. "We might not be out of the woods yet."

"What?"

"Apparently, Reznikov had at least one member of the royal government in his pocket. That's why Scott and the others were forced off the island before they blew the top off the cave."

Charlotte searched the cockpit, then grabbed the pilot's pistol off the deck.

"No," Jason said, waving her off. "We're not engaging in a firefight with the Virgin Islands police. Reznikov and his thugs are done. We need to be diplomatic with these guys if—" He stopped as he watched the bow of the incoming vessel. Scott was leaning against the railing beside two Royal Police Force officers, and he waved as if he knew Jason was looking his way.

Jason chuckled. "I don't know how he does that."

"Does what?" Charlotte asked.

Jason handed her the binoculars, and she focused on the police cruiser. He relaxed a little for the first time in what felt like ages. Seeing their leader on the boat reminded him yet again just how fortunate they were to have the former senator on their side. The man had a way with people and conflict—a knack for coming out on top of any situation, no matter how arduous.

They watched as the sixty-foot police boat pulled along the port side of the drifting aircraft.

Using the gauze and pressure bandages, Charlotte stopped the bleeding from Jason's cuts. He'd be fine for the moment but would need medical attention aboard the *Valiant*.

Charlotte fixed her attention over her shoulder at the approaching patrol boat, then bit her lip. "What happens now?"

Jason didn't have to give the question any thought. "We find your dad."

"But . . . I betrayed you." She dropped her face into her hands. "I betrayed all of you and put your lives in danger."

Jason wrapped an arm around her. "No, Nikolai Reznikov and his band of criminals did that."

Charlotte pressed her head into Jason's chest.

"And you saved my life, Charlotte. Regardless of what you did before, I'd be dead now if it weren't for you, and Reznikov would be flying away with the treasure."

A whistle sounded as the pilot of the patrol boat expertly maneuvered the craft against the forward part of the plane's fuselage. Jason spotted Scott against the ship's starboard railing, the officers beside him holding coiled ropes.

Jason opened the aircraft's side door, waved, then tied two lines cast from the boat's deck.

Scott threw himself over the starboard railing with a big smile on his face. "Hell of a landing, kid," he said, shaking Jason's hand.

"You have no idea how good it is to see you. And how'd you convince the police that we're the good guys? You talk some sense into whoever Reznikov was working with?"

"The man's handcuffed in the brig as we speak. Fortunately, the members of the Royal Police Force have good heads on their shoulders."

"What's gonna happen to him?"

"With our digital proof of his dealings with Reznikov, he'll be sent back to London and tried. Given the severity of the charges and all of the evidence, he's looking at public disgrace, loss of his position, and a good ten years behind bars. Speaking of the Russian criminal"—Scott peered over Jason's shoulder—"where's he at?"

"In the cargo bay. Let's just say he found out the hard way just how heavy Kidd's fortune is."

Charlotte appeared at Jason's back.

"Miss Murchison," Scott said, striding toward her. "It's great to see you made it. Though I expected nothing less given your impressive resume. How did—"

"She was taken by Reznikov and his men," Jason said, shooting the woman a look. "After they blew into the cave. Then she saved my life mid-flight by attacking Reznikov right before he was about to make me the latest victim of his favorite pistol."

They led Scott into the cargo hold, and he froze, lowering his sunglasses as he beheld the Spanish coins spilling out of the pile of chests.

Scott laughed. "Well, that sure isn't something you see every day."

The Royal officers, led by Sergeant Graham, detained the pilots when they came to and loaded them onto the patrol boat.

"I'll make sure all of this gets into the right hands. You two did good," Scott said as he dialed a number on his phone and walked away.

We all did good, Jason thought. *But I'm not done yet.*

"Do you have any idea where they're holding your father?" Jason said.

Charlotte shook her head. "No, Reznikov called the men who are apparently keeping him hostage. I listened while he told them that I'd fulfilled my end of the bargain, but he told them to keep my father prisoner until we landed in South America. He wanted to ensure I didn't try anything."

Jason focused on Reznikov, his pale right hand the only thing visible under the pile of treasure. Climbing over the chests, Jason heaved aside the old wooden boxes, then reached for the Russian's front pockets. Slipping out the man's cellphone, he strode back to Charlotte.

She cocked her head. "You can track the number he called?"

Jason pocketed the phone and motioned toward the open side door. "No, but I know someone who can."

FORTY-FIVE

"**Y**OU SEE ANYONE on the plane?" Finn asked while sitting against one of the trucks just up from the surf.

Alejandra stood closer to the lapping waves and focused through a pair of binoculars. "Nothing yet, but at least the bird's out of the sky."

They both turned as Sherwin approached, jogging down the beach with a backpack slung over his shoulder. After he and Alejandra had helped the injured Finn to the shore, he'd raced to grab his phone from his parked moped.

Heaving for air, Sherwin handed the phone to Alejandra, then rested his hands on his knees. "I think the years are finally catching up with me."

Alejandra placed a quick call to the *Valiant*. When she asked for an update on Scott, the crew informed her that their fearless leader was still aboard the police boat and that they hadn't heard anything from him.

After ending the call, Alejandra watched carefully as the blue and white cabin cruiser closed in on the distant seaplane. It wasn't until the boat turned around to motor up against the aircraft that she recognized Scott standing up on its bow. Their leader wasn't handcuffed, and as the vessel closed in on the plane, she caught a brief glimpse of him climbing over the side. The door of the plane had opened, but from that angle, she couldn't see anyone aboard.

Half an hour later, Scott arrived on the beach, standing in the cockpit of the same Royal Police interceptor that had taken him away over an hour earlier. The backup skiff from the *Valiant* was also ashore, and one of the team's medical technicians was helping Finn onto the boat.

Scott hopped into the splashing water and greeted his team. "You two are some kind of lucky for getting out of that crash with just a broken leg."

Finn winced as he plopped down in the bow of the skiff. "Yeah, well, I might be close to exhausting my nine lives."

"Speaking of nine lives, how's Jase?" Alejandra asked. "Last I saw him, he was being shot at while making a mad climb into the back of that plane."

"He's fine," Scott said. "Banged up, but he'll be all right. He's on the *Valiant* right now getting stitched up."

Scott told them what happened to Reznikov and how the treasure was going to be taken to Setting Point before being ferried to Tortola.

"Safe to say there's going to be more than enough funds to fully restore the damage done to the reefs by the explosions," he continued, fixing his attention on Sherwin. "And hopefully to give this island better facilities and schools. And with the corrupt governor behind bars, I don't think you'll have to worry anymore about suits wanting to buy up your paradise."

Sherwin smiled. "As much as I hate the circumstances that brought you and your team to my island, I'm forever grateful for all you've done."

"It's we who are grateful," Finn said, adjusting his position in the bow. "We couldn't have made a successful attack without your help. And if you hadn't spotted Jason floating out in the water, he'd be a goner by now."

Scott cocked an eyebrow at the Venezuelan.

"Jase will have to tell you the story," Finn added.

"Speak of the devil," Alejandra said as she gazed toward the anchored *Valiant*. "You said he was receiving medical care?"

Scott nodded. "He's there with Miss Murchison. He got beat up pretty bad. I'd say he might even be out for a couple of days, that is, if the stubborn kid can stay still."

"Something tells me he's not on board with the whole 'staying still' idea," Alejandra said.

When Scott tilted his head, Alejandra pointed out beyond the reef. Just as Scott turned and shielded his eyes from the late afternoon sun, a small amphibious aircraft took off from the water just beyond the *Valiant*. The team's custom plane quickly gained altitude and soared west across the sky.

Scott shook his head. "Where the hell is he off to now?"

FORTY-SIX

THREE OF REZNIKOV'S men sat at a table in the dining room of a small house near the edge of the bluff. The leader and biggest of the group spun his phone on the hardwood beside a nickel-plated Smith and Wesson, anxiously awaiting a phone call.

"It's taking too long," a guy to his left grunted.

The short, round-faced man to his right added, "He's right, Vlad. What if he never contacts us? What if he's cutting us out of the deal?"

"Will you two shut up?" Vlad barked. "He'll call. And then we can get rid of this old man and meet up with the others." He jerked his head to the back of the room, where a man with a sack over his head sat tied to a chair.

The leader spun his phone once more, then checked the time.

It's taking too long, he thought, the unpleasant truth elbowing its way back into his mind. *What if—*

His train of thought was interrupted by the humming AC unit just out the back door sputtering, then going silent.

"You've got to be kidding me," Vlad grumbled. He wiped a thin layer of sweat from his arm. Even with the machine running, the cold-weather criminal and his posse had been uncomfortable in the tropical humidity.

Vlad stabbed a finger at the short guy. "Get the hell out there and see what's wrong with it!"

His subordinate sighed then did as instructed, lumbering out the back door.

As he disappeared, the husky man's eyes rested on their captive once again. Since nabbing the professor from his Florida home, they'd flown him on Reznikov's plane to the secluded safe house overlooking empty bays and a never-ending blue beyond. Vlad and his men were tired, hungry, and ready to get a move on.

A quick bullet to the man's head, and I could get the hell out of here, he thought.

Reznikov had called, informing them that the man's daughter had played her part.

So, why did he say to keep him alive? It's only a matter of time before he'll call me back and give the order. So, why wait?

Vlad gripped his pistol, shifted around in the chair, and aimed the barrel straight at their captive.

"What the hell are you doing?" the other criminal said.

Vlad danced his right index finger over the trigger. "Something we should've done hours ago."

"We should wait for Nikolai," the man said, then turned to face the back door. "And where the hell is Igor?" He raised his voice, shouting the man's name, but no reply came.

Vlad ignored his buddy's words, keeping his gaze and aim trained on their prisoner. While debating whether or not to pull the trigger, his phone buzzed in his pocket. "Saved by the bell, old man," he said, placing his weapon on the table and grabbing his phone. His lips formed a sinister smile as he laid eyes on the number on the screen. "But not for long."

Vlad turned away from their captive, sauntered to the front of the room, and faced the dirty window. "Just give me the word, boss, and I'll gladly put this guy down and toss his body over the cliff." The line was quiet. "Boss? You there?"

"You're not killing anyone, dirtbag," a powerful voice said through the speaker.

Vlad's face contorted with equal parts confusion and anger. "Who the hell is this? Where's Nikolai?"

"He's dead. And I'm the guy who killed him." Jason waited a moment to let the revelation settle. "You've got two choices here, bub. Either you and your buddies leave your little hideout right now without touching a hair on Murchison's head, or I'm gonna hand you the last beating of your miserable life."

"Look," Vlad snarled. "I don't know who the hell you are or who the hell you think you're talking to, but the only way this guy's getting out of here is over my dead body. Understand?"

Silence filled the line, followed by the low-pitched hum of a dial tone.

Vlad wiped his mouth, then eyed their hostage.

"Who the hell was that?" Vlad's accomplice said.

Vlad fumed with rage as he stared at their prisoner. "It doesn't matter." He stormed across the room, snatching his pistol as he weaved around the table, and made a beeline for Murchison. "We're killing this man, and then we're out of here. I'm done with this missi—"

The back door slammed open, nearly flying off its hinges as it pounded against the wall. Jason filled the doorway, his Glock 21 raised. Before the big Russian could do anything but gasp, Jason pulled the trigger, sending a .45-caliber round into the guy's gun hand. The bullet tore through Vlad's flesh, and he howled as he relinquished control of his weapon.

The second criminal bore down on Jason from the right, swinging a powerful hook. Jason lurched forward, seized the guy by the back of his neck, and bashed his face into the doorframe.

With his assailant dazed from the blow, Jason finished him off by forcing the thug around, kneeing him in the gut, and breaking his jaw with the side of his Glock. The blur of rapid-fire attacks caused the guy to fall lifelessly to Jason's feet.

Gripping his pistol with two hands, Jason whirled around just in time to see Vlad slip out the front door of the house. Jason sighed, then ambled across the room.

Back outside, Jason watched as Vlad made a mad dash for the cliffs, cradling his bleeding hand and taking intermittent glimpses back toward the house.

Jason raised his weapon and was just about to bury a round between the guy's shoulder blades when his running quarry slipped on the rocks near the edge of the cliff. Vlad let out a primal shriek as his body vanished over the edge, freefalling to the raging surf.

When Jason reached the rim of the imposing, rocky bluff, he spotted Vlad's corpse facedown, sprawled out over a jagged boulder.

Back at the house, Jason ensured that the area was clear before striding toward the hostage.

"Who's there?" the man said in a calm, intelligent English accent.

"My name is Jason Wake. I've come to get you out of here."

Jason removed the sack, revealing a man in his fifties with a tanned complexion and thinning dark hair. The guy gazed through slits for a moment, blinking as his eyes adjusted to the brightness.

Holstering his pistol, Jason gripped his dive knife and made quick work of the knots securing the captive to the chair. "I'm here with your daughter," he added, helping Murchison to his feet and getting him a bottle of water from a nearby refrigerator.

"Charlotte's here?" he said, scanning the room.

Jason nodded, then motioned toward the back door. Murchison chugged half the water, then followed Jason through the doorway, past the sabotaged AC unit and the motionless first criminal.

Jason guided him down a narrow, quarter-mile footpath along the top of the cliff before cutting down toward a beach in North Side Bay. As they neared the shore, Charlotte appeared, bounding from beside Jason's amphibious aircraft and sprinting across the white sand. Though beyond weary, her father also took off, and the two met in a long embrace, both shedding tears of joy.

After a minute of emotional chatter, Charlotte waved Jason over. "Jason Wake," she said, wiping tears from her cheeks. "I'd like you to meet my father, Frank Murchison."

Jason shook his hand. "It's a pleasure, sir. Charlotte's told me a lot about you."

"The pleasure is mine. How can I ever thank you for saving my life?"

"And saving mine," Charlotte added.

Jason thought for a moment, then gestured toward the plane. "I'd love for you two to join me for dinner tonight. You must be starving after the last twenty-four hours you've had, and I know a place just a quick flight away that grills some of the best lobster in the Caribbean."

Frank smiled, then patted Jason on the back. "I must say, you make one hell of a first impression."

FORTY-SEVEN

THE TIRED SUN hung low on the western horizon, emitting brilliant streaks of light over the Caribbean. Touching down off the northwestern edge of Anegada, Jason slowed and eased the amphibious aircraft's hull against the wooden planks of the dock stretching out in front of Potter's by the Sea.

After shutting down the engine and tying off, Jason, Charlotte, and Frank strode down the wharf and were welcomed by the happiest group of islanders any of them had ever seen.

Henrietta, having spotted their arrival first, met them at the steps with fully outstretched arms. "Sherwin's been talking my ears off for the last hour about you two."

"And it still isn't enough to do them justice," Sherwin said, raising his drink and lumbering over to greet the arrivals.

Jason introduced Frank, then moved to a big table against the railing.

"Nice of you to drop by," Scott said, patting Jason on the shoulder. "And thanks for the heads-up."

"I had some final business to take care of."

"And someone to pick up, apparently," Finn said, motioning toward Frank.

Jason introduced him to the group, and Scott gravitated toward Murchison.

"Small world, professor," Scott said, shaking Frank's hand. "I'm sorry you were caught up in this mess."

"I wish I could say it was the first time I've been taken hostage by bad guys. Thankfully, I wasn't prisoner for long, and thankfully Jason here is proficient at delivering beatdowns."

"You two know each other?" Jason said, raising his eyebrows.

He was left speechless by the connection. Everywhere they went, their leader seemed to know someone.

"We've met a couple of times," Scott said, the two men exchanging knowing glances. "Perhaps it's fate that a famous golden-age pirate treasure caused our paths to cross yet again."

Frank crinkled his brow. "Did you say a pirate treasure?"

"It's Captain Kidd's, dad," Charlotte said, striding forward. "And you should see it. It's incredible and was found in a cave on the other side of the island." She turned to Scott. "Is there any way we could examine it? Valuable items like that deserve proper care, as much as that ship has already sailed, thanks to Reznikov's boys."

"The chests are being taken to Tortola as we speak," Scott said. "There, the local government will disperse it as they see fit." He motioned toward a lean, middle-aged woman seated across from him. "Mrs. Jaqueline Frazer, Anegada's district representative, is leading the charge. Jackie, I'm sure you wouldn't mind if Charlotte and Frank lend a hand . . ."

"It would be our honor," she said enthusiastically. "And perhaps one day we can create a museum here on the island dedicated to the famous pirate and his incredible story and treasure."

Elvis emptied the trap of lobster, and the restaurant's animated cook grilled up the whole batch and then carried them out on trays. The mouthwatering aroma wafted across the porch, and the group dined on the fresh seafood while watching Mother Nature put on a majestic display. An ever-shifting palette of vibrant reds, oranges, yellows, and pinks illuminated the sky, and the group stared in awe at the spellbinding work of art, basking in the final rays that glistened across the calm bay. When the last remnants of the glowing orb vanished, the group let out a cheer and drank in honor of the day.

After sunset, the night really heated up as they enjoyed fresh coconut tart and lime pie for dessert, and drank while Elvis belted out off-key versions of Marley hits. It was intimate in that kind of way when strangers gather due to a common cause, and it was well after midnight when the party dissipated.

As Alejandra helped a hobbling Finn to their tied-off boat, Scott approached Jason.

"We're gonna head to Tortola to make sure everything's handled smoothly with the governor and treasure," Scott said.

"I'll meet you there in a couple days," Jason replied.

"You don't wanna come with us?"

"I was thinking of staying here for a bit. Maybe enjoy the island while not having to worry about crazy criminals raining on the parade."

"Careful," Sherwin said, overhearing the conversation. "Anegada is like the sirens from 'Homer's Odyssey.' The island's beauty is enchanting, and she could hold you in her grasp for life. And if you're looking for somewhere to holiday, there's no better place to savor the vibrations than at the beach club."

Scott patted Jason on the back again. "Just don't let the sirens seduce you for too long. Our operation isn't much useful without the tip of its spear."

"Do me a favor and snag one of Kidd's coins for me, will you?"

Scott grinned. "I'll see what I can do."

As the place cleared out, Jason made his way to the end of the dock, relishing the serenity and the cool breeze off the water. Charlotte eventually approached, and they stood in silence a moment, looking out at the dark harbor.

"So," Charlotte said, wrapping an arm around him. "What's next for Jason Wake?"

Jason's aching body answered the question for him. "I think I might need to relax for a couple of days before I figure that one out. What about you?"

"Well, after I take a closer look at the treasure, I was thinking the same thing. You have anywhere particular in mind for that relaxing?"

Jason smiled. Before he could reply, Frank approached them from down the dock.

"I wanted to thank you again before I leave, Jason," he said. "I fear that those criminals were moments away from pulling the trigger when you arrived."

"After everything your daughter did to help our group, it was the least I could do. Reznikov was willing to stoop to low depths to get what he wanted. Fortunately, we won't have to worry about him anymore."

Frank nodded. "I'm heading to Tortola with Scott." He motioned toward the boat tied off two docks down, and Charlotte told him that she'd be right there.

"I can only spare two days, then I must return home," Frank added. "Jason, if you're ever in the Florida Keys, don't hesitate to drop a line. I spend much of the year there teaching at a local college in Key West."

"I have friends in Key West," Jason replied. "Logan Dodge and his family showed me around their paradise earlier this year."

"You know Logan? Well, small world indeed."

As he walked off, Jason shifted his attention back out over the water.

Charlotte bit her lip. "I still don't understand how you've forgiven me so easily. You could've died because of what I did to help Nikolai. You *and* your team."

By way of an answer, and to fully convince Charlotte he'd forgiven her, Jason closed the distance and soared in for a kiss. Unable to control herself, Charlotte pushed forward, and their lips met. The act sent a rush across Jason's body, a surge of passion punctuating the past week and the long day they'd had.

Jason pulled back and gazed into her moonlit eyes, then caught sight of the boat as the group prepared to shove off.

"I'm hoping that was a sample of what's to come . . ." Charlotte said.

Jason kissed her forehead. "You know where to find me."

FORTY-EIGHT

JASON TOOK SHERWIN up on his suggestion and gave his body and mind a much-needed rest at the Anegada Beach Club.

The owner happily welcomed him to the quiet getaway on the island's northern coast. "Sherwin called and said you'd be stopping by," he said, shaking Jason's hand. "I have a special place for you. One of our most popular tents."

At first, Jason thought the guy was pulling his leg. Though he enjoyed camping, sleeping in a tiny polyester dome wasn't exactly the restful getaway he'd had in mind.

The owner led him down a sandy footpath, then pointed toward a beautifully modern but rustic palapa resting on the slope of a sand dune just steps from the unspoiled beach. He followed the islander up onto the sturdy wooden base and the private porch that offered sweeping views of the turquoise Caribbean. With hammocks swaying on the covered deck, canvas walls to allow the breeze to pass through, and comfortable furnishings under a palm-thatched roof, the place left Jason speechless.

"This will work?" the owner said with a broad smile.

Jason nodded. "Yeah, this'll work."

He spent the next two days lounging in the hammocks, dining on the restaurant's fresh seafood, and resting on the plush mattress to the sound of nearby lapping surf. Wanting to take in the local scenery without worrying about the potential threat of danger, he spent hours freediving up and down the coast and out to the nearby reefs. It was paradise on earth, and on the evening of the second day, it got even better.

While splashing through the shallows, his fins in one hand and his mask in the other, Jason spotted a woman strolling down the shore in a yellow and white sundress. Squinting, he blocked out the late-day sunshine and beamed when he realized it was Charlotte.

"You look like a different man," she said when her toes hit the water.

"Look who's talking." He motioned over his shoulder at the azure Shangri-la at his back. "Care for a swim?"

"Aren't you tired?"

"I think I could suck it up for another round."

The two waded out into the shallows, and Jason showed her the reef—the impossibly vibrant colors, the abundance of marine life of every shape and size, and the unique features of coral and limestone. With the sun sinking into the ocean, they scampered to shore, racing each other up onto the porch of Jason's palapa. Unable to keep their hands off each other, they stumbled to the hardwood floor at the foot of the bed, their soaked bodies pressed tight against each other and their lips locked. They made love with the last glows of sunlight shooting beams across the sky. Then, after a late dinner, they showered and passed out in each other's arms.

For three days, they lounged and snorkeled and savored each other's company. They talked for hours about everything, from how Kidd's treasure was being dealt with to their distinctly unique childhoods. On the fourth day, they kayaked to the western tip and snorkeled in a slice of Heaven with no other human in sight for miles.

When they arrived back at the room, Charlotte stepped out to the porch. She paced back and forth with her phone glued to her ear as Jason showered, then she met him inside.

"I hate to say this, but it looks like our getaway has to come to an end." She glanced at her phone. "A colleague needs my help with a project."

"Leaving me already, huh? I knew you were out of my league from the start."

She chuckled, then moved in for a quick kiss. "That mean you want to see me again? I'll be back home in Boston for a few months. I could show you around."

Jason considered the offer. He'd enjoyed the company of great women over the past six months, but what he had with Charlotte felt different. For the first time in nearly two years, he felt a foreign yet friendly desire to press on and see where the road led.

Jason shrugged. "I'll have to check in with the team first, but if there aren't any pressing matters, sure, I'll swing by."

Charlotte looked at him like he was crazy. "I was kidding. You've got this beautiful tropical paradise nearly to yourself, and you want to leave it for New England?"

Jason kissed her on the forehead, then made his way down her cheek. "Sure, as long as you don't leave me until tomorrow."

Early the next morning, Jason returned from a spearfishing jaunt out to the reef to find a text message from Scott that said to call him right away.

"Nice haul," the owner of the resort said, sauntering down the beach and pulling Jason's attention from the screen.

Jason slid a mesh bag from his shoulder holding a barracuda and two yellowtail snappers. He hung the fish on a hook, along with his mask and fins, and rested his pole spear against the side of the palapa. "It's easy in these waters. You guys are spoiled."

The islander grinned. "We are, indeed."

As Charlotte appeared from inside the cottage and admired the catch, Jason excused himself and trekked up the nearest sand dune. Still clutching his phone, he called his mentor.

"You still on Anegada?" Scott said in a firm tone.

"Time flies here."

"Well, I hate to rain on your parade, kid, but we've been called up to the big leagues. I just got off the phone with the president."

Jason squinted as he reached the top of the rise. "Whose president?"

"Ours. We've been requested to aid in an urgent matter of global security based on the CIA deputy director's recommendation. Our team's heading north, right away."

"Where to?"

"Iceland."

"That's north all right. What's going on?"

Scott paused. "A team of experts on a scientific expedition were attacked. I'll brief you when you get here. This is highly time sensitive, Jase."

"Roger that, Scottie."

Jason hung up and hustled down the dune. As he rushed up the palapa's steps, he gestured toward the owner. "Fish are all yours."

THE END

ALSO BY MATTHEW RIEF

FLORIDA KEYS ADVENTURE SERIES:

Featuring Logan Dodge

Gold in the Keys
Hunted in the Keys
Revenge in the Keys
Betrayed in the Keys
Redemption in the Keys
Corruption in the Keys
Predator in the Keys
Legend in the Keys
Abducted in the Keys
Showdown in the Keys
Avenged in the Keys
Broken in the Keys
Payback in the Keys

JASON WAKE NOVELS

Caribbean Wake
Surging Wake
Relentless Wake

JOIN THE ADVENTURE!

Sign up for my newsletter to receive updates on upcoming books on my website:

MATTHEWRIEF.COM

ABOUT THE AUTHOR

MATTHEW HAS A deep-rooted love for adventure and the ocean. He loves traveling, diving, rock climbing and writing adventure novels. Though he grew up in the Pacific Northwest, he currently lives in Virginia Beach with his wife, Jenny.

Made in the USA
Monee, IL
05 May 2023